HARBINGERS 20

End Game

Alton Gansky

Bill Myers, Jeff Gerke
and Angela Hunt

Published by Amaris Media International.
Copyright © 2017 Alton Gansky
Cover Design: Angela Hunt

ISBN-13: 978-1546334927
ISBN-10: 1546334920

For more information, visit us on Facebook:
https://www.facebook.com/pages/Harbingers/705107309586877

or _www.harbingersseries.com_.

HARBINGERS

A novella series by
Bill Myers, Frank Peretti, Jeff Gerke, Angela Hunt,
and Alton Gansky

In this fast-paced world with all its demands, the five of us wanted to try something new. Instead of the longer novel format, we wanted to write something equally as engaging but that could be read in one or two sittings—on the plane, waiting to pick up the kids from soccer, or as an evening's read.

We also wanted to play. As friends and seasoned novelists, we thought it would be fun to create a game we could participate in together. The rules were simple:

Rule #1
Each of us will write as if we were one of the characters in the series:

Bill Myers will write as Brenda, the street-hustling

tattoo artist who sees images of the future.

Frank Peretti will write as the professor, the atheist ex-priest ruled by logic.

Jeff Gerke will write as Chad, the mind reader with devastating good looks and an arrogance to match.

Angela Hunt will write as Andi, the brilliant-but-geeky young woman who sees inexplicable patterns.

Alton Gansky will write as Tank, the naïve, big-hearted jock with a surprising connection to a healing power.

Rule #2

Instead of the five of us writing one novella together (we're friends but not crazy), we would write it like a TV series. There would be an overarching storyline into which we'd plug our individual novellas, with each story written from our character's point of view.

If you're keeping track, this is the order:

Harbingers #1—*The Call*—Bill Myers
Harbingers #2—*The Haunted*—Frank Peretti
Harbingers #3—*The Sentinels*—Angela Hunt
Harbingers #4—*The Girl*—Alton Gansky

Volumes #1-4 omnibus: *Cycle One: Invitation*

Harbingers #5—*The Revealing*—Bill Myers
Harbingers #6—*Infestation*—Frank Peretti
Harbingers #7—*Infiltration*—Angela Hunt
Harbingers #8—*The Fog*—Alton Gansky

Volumes #5-8 omnibus: *Cycle Two: The Assault*

Harbingers #9—*Leviathan*—Bill Myers
Harbingers #10—*The Mind Pirates*—Frank Peretti
Harbingers #11—*Hybrids*—Angela Hunt
Harbingers #12—*The Village*—Alton Gansky

Volumes 9-12 omnibus: *Cycle Three: Probing*

Harbingers #13—*Piercing the Veil*—Bill Myers
Harbingers #14—*Home Base*—Jeff Gerke
Harbingers #15—*Fairy*—Angela Hunt
Harbingers #16—*At Sea*—Alton Gansky

Volumes 13-16 omnibus: *Cycle Four: The Pursuit*

Harbingers #17—*Piercing the Veil*—Bill Myers
Harbingers #18—*Interesting Times*—Jeff Gerke
Harbingers #19—*Into the Blue*—Angela Hunt
Harbingers #20—*End Game*—Alton Gansky

There you have it. We hope you'll find these as entertaining in the reading as we are in the writing.

Bill, Frank, Jeff, Angie, and Al

TUNNEL OF LOVE

My name is Tank and this is the story of my death.

I hate to start things off with such a bummer, but such is life ... or in this case, death.

To be honest, I'm not very surprised by my loomin' demise. I've known it was comin' for a long time. To be honest again, I'm a little surprised I've lasted this long. If you've followed my—I should say, *our*—adventures over the last two years or so, then you know I've been called on to jump off a high-rise building, fight off a beast that wasn't nuthin' but fur, claws, bloody teeth, and meanness. I've faced off with flying orbs that meant the world no good, demonic critters, and a dozen other unbelievable horrors, many of which visit me in my dreams (although until now

I've refused to mention it). I've lived through about nineteen such missions. Sometimes I come through without so much as a scratch; other times I've nearly bought the farm. But God has been good to me, to us, and I spring back. In each of those impossible cases, I've faced death with at least a spoonful of optimism.

But not this time.

I'm stuck in a dark tunnel beneath the ice of the Antarctic. Our space is lit by a single flashlight. We each have lights, but we're tryin' to save the batteries.

I'm not alone. Sitting next to me is my friend— Since I'm about to check out of this life, I might as well just say it—my friend and the girl I love, Andi Goldstein. We've never kissed, never held hands in a romantic way, never said the things lovers say. She has kept her distance; kept our relationship professional. I learned to live with it. But now that we've probably come to the end of the road, she has pulled down the barriers. She sits on the ice floor next to me. Close. She holds my arm. My dream for so long. So very long.

Brenda is here, her head hung low, her arms wrapped around her adopted son, Daniel. Daniel is my little buddy and he may be the smartest and most powerful of us all. Looking at him now presses my heart through a meat grinder.

Chad stood off by himself muttering and pacing. He's changed in the last hour. He's a different man.

The professor is with us. *Was* with us. He had been absent for so long, but he came back. He too was a different man. I say *was* because I just watched him sacrifice his life for us. Honorable to the end. And a very brave man.

Also with us is Zeke—a red-headed navy guy with classic movie hero looks and build. He is our guide. Boy, did he choose poorly. Zeke has spent the last half-hour trying to radio the surface. We had descended over a thousand feet through an ice shaft drilled for that purpose. Radio contact would have been pretty easy if moving ice over our heads hadn't crushed the shaft and sheared off our communication line.

At the end of the tunnel waits Azazel, an evil creature that is as old as the earth itself. Maybe older. He killed the professor. He did more than kill him: He crucified the old man and there was nothing we could do about it but run.

So here we are. Our exit iced in. There are only two choices. Sit here and die, or go back down the long ice tunnel to Azazel's domain and face off with a creature the world has not seen since before Noah's flood.

Death waits for us here.

Death waits for us there.

So there you have it.

I do the impossible. I pull myself away from Andi and rise. My joints are stiff from the cold. We all wear the latest in cold weather gear but it can't keep us warm forever.

I cleared my throat. "This is where I usually say something encouraging. I got nuthin'." I looked down the ice tunnel. "Best I can tell, this is the end of the line for us." Those words barely made it past my lips. "But you know me. I was born without the ability to give up, so I gotta do somethin'. I don't want to die sitting on my butt." I picked up my backpack. We still have our gear and our explosives. I'm going to go back to the chamber and let Azazel know my opinion of him.

Andi rose with a grunt. "I'm going with you."

"I can do it by myself." I couldn't tear my gaze from her.

She stepped close, leaned in and kissed me. My heart ground to a stop. I couldn't breathe. I didn't care. I returned the kiss. For a long moment, I was in heaven; and for that same long moment, I was all warm and toasty inside.

She pulled away, and stroked my cheek. "I wasn't asking permission, Tank. I was informing you."

That was my Andi. Smart. Able to see patterns in anything and everything, but she wasn't too good on taking orders from anybody, especially me.

"I'm going too," Chad said. "I can't let Sweet Cheeks—"

I cut him a glance that was colder than the ice that threatened to swallow us. He liked to call Andi Sweet Cheeks and put the moves on her. He was, or had been, a lady's man. He got no encouragement from Andi, and I sure wasn't gonna encourage him. I hated the pet name Sweet Cheeks more than Andi did, and she despised it.

Chad cleared his throat. "I mean, I can't let Andi show me up. Bad for my ego."

Daniel rose from the ice and started for me.

"What do you think you're doing?" Brenda snapped.

Daniel shrugged. "There's only one way out, Mom, and Tank is gonna blow it up. I wanna see."

"No, you're not. You're gonna stay right here with me."

Daniel shuffled a few feet in her direction, but

stopped before reaching her. "Mom, what difference does it make?"

Brenda shook her head, but it lasted only a moment. There was no arguing with her boy. She pushed to her feet. "Fine. Just fine."

Zeke grabbed his backpack. "Okay, it's a party then."

That was good to see. Zeke had a special job to do, and we all knew it.

"Before we go make martyrs of ourselves, Cowboy," Brenda said. "Maybe you could, you know, say a prayer or something."

Brenda had never asked for prayer before.

Never.

Ever.

So I prayed.

"I'm the worst mother ever," Brenda said after my *amen*.

You gotta understand something about our team. We each have powers we never asked for and go off on missions for a group we call the Watchers; missions nobody with half a brain would consider. Still, we go. We go because we know the world needs us to go, even though most of the time we don't know why. Over time, we've learned a few things, but we don't know what all the connections are. The one thing we *do* know, we're fighting an evil that ain't good for the world and the people who live in it.

"I hate missions like this." Chad stepped to my side and looked down the ice corridor to the faint light in the distance. There was an extra measure of fear in his voice. He was bold, brash, mouthy, arrogant, and full of himself. But he was also smart and tuned into everything around him. A late addition to our team—a replacement for the professor who had gone missing for quite a while—he had managed to tick off everyone in the team but Daniel. He also did more to pull us into a team than any one of us could have managed.

I was pretty sure I knew what he meant, but I took the bait. "Missions like what?"

"Oh, you know, the ones with monsters and ghouls and screaming and pain and blood and no hope of survival. Missions with no way out and no way of succeeding."

"Yeah," I said. "We've had a few of those."

More quiet. We stood like a pile of stones. I should take the first few steps down the path. The others would follow me. I knew that, but my feet wouldn't move.

"I assume you got a plan, Cowboy." Brenda's normal cockiness was missing. None of us was feeling any too cocky.

"Well?" Chad asked. "How 'bout it, big guy? What's the play?"

My original thought was simple. I was thinking of taking one of the backpacks full of explosives and putting all my football training to use. The answer seemed obvious: set the charges and run for Azazel's throne room, bulldozing through anyone or anything that stood in my way. The bombs would go off and that would be the end of Azazel and his under-ice lair.

Or would it?

"Somethin' ain't right," I said.

"Duh. You think?" Chad relapsed into his forever annoying self. "Nothing about this is right. If that thing is what Andi says it is, a fallen angel, then there's a very good chance our explosives aren't going to kill him and his buddies. I mean, can angels die?"

"Probably not," I said. "The Bible never mentions dead angels, just angels in heaven and angels bound—"

"Mom?"

I didn't like the sound of Daniel's voice. It was drippin' with concern. I looked behind me, expecting to see Brenda standing within arm's reach of Daniel.

A moment ago she was on her feet, now she sat on the ice, hunched over the ice floor and running her fingers over the uneven surface.

"Mom, what's wrong?" Daniel stepped to his adopted mother. She didn't look up.

That was unusual. Brenda loved that boy so much I think she would have carried him in a pocket if she could get him to fit.

She cocked her head to one side, then snapped it back up.

"She sees something," Andi said.

The only light came from the one flashlight, its beam reflecting off the scalloped ice. Time to burn a few more electrons, or photons, or both. I clicked on my light and directed the beam to Brenda's face. She didn't react, didn't lift her head. She kept her gaze down on the ice. I shone my light at the ice in front of her.

"I don't see anything," I said.

"Not on the ice, Big Guy, in her head." Andi moved to Brenda's pack and retrieved a small sketch pad. Brenda always had a sketch pad. She'd sooner go out in public without her clothes than leave the house without something to draw on.

Andi knelt at Brenda's side and held the pad up for Brenda to see. "Here you go, girlfriend—"

Brenda snatched it before Andi could finish her sentence. Brenda began patting her parka like a nicotine addict looking for a smoke.

"Here." Andi retrieved a pencil from Brenda's back pack. Brenda snapped that up, too.

"Is this how she normally works?" Zeke asked.

"Not usually." I moved a couple of steps closer to Brenda and directed my light on the pad, though I had no doubt she could have drawn her mental image in the pitch dark. "She gets pretty lost in the process, but this is over the top for even her." I didn't bother mentioning that I bear one of Brenda's tattoos on my arm. That's what started this whole thing.

We gathered around our friend and kept our mouths shut.

Whatever Brenda draws tends to come true. In a sense, she sees the future. She's almost always right, and the few times events didn't match up was because we had done something to change the future. Andi said it was like in that story by Dickens, *A Christmas Carol.* Scrooge is visited by three ghosts and shown his past, the present, and future. When he saw the future, he asked the ghost if what he saw was what *could* be or what *had* to be. He wanted to know if he could change his own destiny.

Sometimes we change the future. I didn't want to say it out loud, but I was praying she was drawing something that showed a better outcome than the last one she drew—the one that showed all of us except Daniel dead. I would really enjoy seeing somethin' else.

I leaned over Brenda and stared at her drawing. She had made short work of the image. After several moments of studying the lines she had penciled on the paper, I wished she had spent a little more time on the work. Normally we had no problem figuring out what she meant.

Not this time.

Chapter 2

DRAW ME A PICTURE

"Anyone want tell me what I'm lookin' at?" I kept my light on the sketch pad.

No one spoke. At least not at first.

"I got no clue." Brenda was back with us. "I take it I zoned out a bit?"

"A bit?" Chad said.

Brenda studied the image she had drawn. "Don't ask. I don't know."

"It just looks like a bunch of parallel lines," Chad

said. "Well, they're not all parallel, but each line has a companion."

I looked at Andi. "You got anythin'?"

"Yeah, Pattern-Girl," Brenda said. "I draw 'em; you interpret them."

Enough light spilled over for me to see Andi shake her head. She hated it when Brenda called her Pattern-Girl. It sounded too much like the name of some comic book hero.

Andi reached for the pad. "Let me take a closer look."

"Sure, but someone help me up, this ice is freezing my tochus." Brenda handed the sketch pad to Andi and I helped our frozen artist to her feet.

"I need more light, Tank."

"Glad to oblige." I moved to Andi's side and stood close. I didn't need to be that close to shine my light on the paper, but…hey, it's Andi.

Andi held the drawing at arm's length. She tilted her head from one side to another, then tilted the pad. More than once she had found patterns in things; patterns that helped us, even saved a life or two.

"See anythin'?"

"Hush, Tank. Let me think."

I hushed.

A moment later she nodded. "Maybe. Possibly. Perhaps. Yes." She raised her gaze. "Zeke, I want you to look at this."

Zeke was a navy man and clearly used to taking orders. He stepped in close enough to see Brenda's sketch.

"What do you think?" Andi tilted the pad in his direction.

"Think? I don't think anything. It's a bunch of almost straight lines."

"It's more than that," Andi said. "Chad is right. Many of the lines run parallel to another line, but notice the line weights."

"Lines have weight?" I felt stupid for asking, but I was used to showing off my ignorance.

"Artists make some lines thin and light, other lines mighty thick," Brenda answered. "You make the thick lines by pressing harder on your pencil, or pen, or whatever you're usin'."

"Oh." It was all I had.

"Wait a sec," Zeke said. "Some of this looks familiar." He pinched the bridge of his nose as if squeezing a memory into his brain. A second or two later he snapped his head up and looked at Andi. He smiled.

"Tunnels." They said the word in unison.

"Exactly," Zeke said. "These are like what we've seen on ice-penetrating radar. Except—"

Uh-oh. "Except what?" I asked.

"Except they're not the same. Just similar. Of course, even as good as those instruments are, they might have missed something."

"Or whoever provided the readings messed with them," Chad said.

Zeke didn't bother to look up from the drawing. "You're a tad paranoid, aren't you?"

"Yep. Paranoid people are paranoid because they pay attention."

Zeke nodded. "Point taken. I suppose someone could have tampered with the info I was given. There's no way to know."

"That doesn't really matter," I said. "We are where

we are. The question is why Brenda drew this now."

"Apparently," Andi said, "we need to change our plans. Instead of storming Azazel's space, we take a different tunnel and see where it leads."

"Makes sense to me," Chad said. "I wasn't real keen about going back there."

It was starting to make sense to me. Our goal was to do in Azazel. I doubted we could do that. Like I mentioned earlier, there is no mention of dead angels in the Bible. So, since we can't end Azazel, we could end the usefulness of this base. That's what we came to do. That's what we needed to do.

"Okay," I said. "How do we find the tunnel?"

More silence. I hated that kind of silence. It meant none of us had a clue about what to do next.

Andi studied the drawing again. "Brenda, why couldn't you add a *You Are Here* sign or something?"

"Really? You gonna blame me?"

Andi stepped to her and gave her a hug. "No way, girl. I'm just a little frustrated. Okay, I'm a *lot* frustrated and more than a little scared."

"I hear that," Brenda said.

"We go up the tunnel," Zeke said, sounding like the captain of a ship.

"Why?" I asked.

"Because we've already gone the other way and didn't see anything that might lead us to the tunnels in this drawing."

He had me there. "Okay, so you're our guide. Take the lead. I'll bring up the rear."

Daniel giggled. "You said *rear*."

That kid has the strangest sense of humor.

Zeke grabbed his pack of explosives. The rest of us picked up our packs and we all marched in the opposite direction.

**

We trudged on with Zeke in the lead and me in the rear constantly looking over my shoulder. My brain kept telling me that Azazel's minions didn't need to bother with us. We had no way to the surface. Sooner, rather than later, we would freeze. Our clothing would keep us warm for a good while, but all the space age materials and designs wouldn't keep our hearts beating for long. Just breathing in the cold air hurt.

Andi hung back until I caught up to her. The tunnel was narrowing, but we could still walk side by side. She took my hand. That warmed my heart and I wished we were someplace where we could hold hands without arctic gloves on.

"You doing okay?" she asked.

"I'm doing. How about you?"

"About the same." She squeezed my hand. "You're my hero. You know that, right? You have been for a long time. It took me awhile to realize it, but I figured I would have time to sort out my emotions. Turns out, I was wrong. Watching the professor die made me realize that any of us could be next. And if Brenda's drawing—"

"Maybe that will change."

"Maybe. Maybe."

I could tell she had serious doubts about changing Brenda's prophecy of our death. Sure, we had altered such predictions in the past, but this one felt different. We all seemed to feel that.

"Anyway," Andi said, "I want you to know I regret

keeping you at a distance."

"No problem. I'm a patient man."

"Let a girl apologize, Big Guy."

"Sorry." And I was.

"I know you've taken some ribbing about your faith. The professor was the worse until, you know, he went away. He found his faith again. To think he spent so much time trying to prove there was no God only to learn there was."

She paused and I didn't interrupt her silence. A lot can be said in silence.

Then she started again. "From priest to rationalistic atheist back to man of faith. I didn't see that coming."

I shrugged. "He had seen too much of the supernatural to deny it any more. We all have. It's only by the grace of God we're still here."

"Where will the grace of God be when the end comes for us?"

"Sometimes death is a grace, Andi. No one lives this life forever."

"How do you hang on, Tank? You never seem to stumble, never lose faith."

I put my arm around her. She seemed smaller than usual, frailer. "I have my days. I . . . Do you remember when that fairy creature—the one with the scorpion tail—stung Daniel?"

"How could I not? I can still hear him scream."

"Me, too. I love that kid." Then came the words hard for me to say. "When I saw that—when I heard his pain—well, it still haunts me. The sight and sound of my little buddy writhing in such agony…"

My voice broke. I took a minute to stuff my feelings so I could get on with things. "Anyway, me and the good Lord had a few conversations. I did all the talking. He did the listening. I couldn't explain why the innocent suffer so much."

"Did He answer your doubts?"

"I wouldn't call them *doubts*. I was angry with God. That happens to Christians. Our ignorance gets in the way of understanding. Truth is, no one has all the answers."

"So, you didn't get a response?"

"Not like most people would expect. But I came to understand something important. I'm not deep like some people. Compared to the professor, you, and Chad, I'm a bit of a mental lightweight, but occasionally I trip over something important. It's not like a revelation in the Bible, but it is a revelation to me."

"And what is that?"

I took a deep breath. "Every ending is a beginning."

Chapter 3

A TIGHT FIT

"Bingo!"

Zeke's voice rolled down the tunnel.

Andi and I rushed forward. Zeke and Chad were standing by a vertical fissure in the ice wall of the tunnel. A good thing, because the tunnel ended just a few yards ahead.

Zeke used his flashlight to examine the crack in the wall.

"Whatya see?" Brenda asked. "Will it get us back to the surface?"

"Not that I can see, but I can make out a few things." Zeke leaned into the opening. "I make the opening to be about thirty inches wide—just like the shaft we used to get down here. It's also about seven or eight feet tall. The floor slopes down some. Not enough to be a problem."

"Just thirty inches?" I said. I had had all I wanted of narrow passageways. My size is great for football, not so great for squeezing through things.

"At best, Tank. Sorry." Zeke studied the opening a few more moments, then stepped back and removed his backpack. "I'll be right back."

Chad took the pack and set it on the ice floor. Zeke slipped into the opening carrying only his flashlight.

"I can feel a bit of a breeze," he called. "A good sign. It means we have air flow."

I stood by the opening listening to Zeke chatter and huff and puff. I could tell he was making progress. I could also tell it was not easy going.

"Almost at the end. Stand by."

Chad looked at me and shrugged. "Where else would we go?"

"I'm in." Zeke's voice sounded distant, but it was loud enough to generate an echo.

Then nothing. A minute passed. Two.

I stuck my head in the fissure. "Zeke?"

Nothing.

Great. I began to ponder what to do if Zeke didn't come back. On the plus side of things, I hadn't heard any blood-curdling screams.

"Is he okay, Cowboy?"

I turned to Brenda. I wanted to say, "How should I know?" but I refrained. Instead, I admitted that I didn't know. "Let's give him a little time. He knows what he's doing."

"Really?" Chad said. "*None* of us know what we're doing. This whole thing has been played by ear."

I hate it when Chad is right.

I heard a distant grunt, some scraping, some heavy breathing. A few moments later Zeke's smiling face appeared, then he oozed out of the opening.

"Well, that was fun." He was breathing heavily. "Good thing I'm not claustrophobic."

I wasn't in the mood for chitchat. "Whatcha see?"

"The fissure appears to be a natural break in the ice, not manmade. There's a chamber on the other side. It's about the size of a master bedroom. And it's closed in on all sides."

"So, no tunnel?" Andi said.

"There's a tunnel, but it's not all that easy to reach. The floor of the tunnel doesn't align with the floor of the chamber. The opening is about seven feet up. I was able to pull myself part way up, but couldn't hang on to the ice very long. I did take a quick look at the tunnel and it's plenty wide. Best I could tell from that glance, it's a natural fissure, maybe from a trickle of water at a time when this place was warmer."

"Which way does it go?" Chad pressed.

"Same direction we came from, but I think it slopes downward. If the slope holds, it might go even deeper than Azazel's throne room. Maybe."

"You mean . . . it might be a way to get beneath butt-ugly's chamber?" Chad has a way with words.

"I can't say for sure. There's only one way to find out. Whacha say?"

Chad shrugged. "I got no plans for my day."

Zeke looked at me. "Tank?"

I took a silent poll of the others. No one argued against the idea, and how could they? There wasn't anything else we could do. "I say we go. We have a mission to complete."

Zeke straightened, then took a deep breath. "Here's the thing, Tank. I can fit through again. Everyone else here is smaller and thinner than I am. Everyone but you. It's gonna be the shaft problem all over again."

We had been lowered one by one through a thirty-inch shaft. It worked great for everyone but me. I got stuck. I was left with only one solution; I had to melt some of the ice. We all have our gifts, all but Zeke, and mine is healing—a very hit-and-miss gift. Sometimes it works; often it doesn't. When I lay hands on someone, my hands get warm. That heat was enough to help me make the descent. Barely. I had no guarantees that it would work in this situation.

"I'll make it." I said those words like I fully believed them. "How do you want to do this?"

Zeke thought for a moment. "I'll go through first. Once I'm part way through send Andi—"

"No." Andi said the word in way that meant she wasn't about to debate. "Chad next, then Brenda and Daniel. I'll go through with Tank."

"Andi," I began. "It might be better—"

"Again, Tank, I'm not asking permission, I'm informing you."

That line had lost its humor, but I knew enough not to argue. Apparently, Zeke and the others agreed.

***

I watched Zeke disappear into the fissure again. It

was like watching a wall of ice swallow him. I stood by the opening, straining my ears to hear every breath the man took.

A few minutes oozed like hours before I heard, "Half way. Next."

"You're up, Chad," I said.

"You know something," Chad said as he stepped into the opening. "This is one crazy job we have."

"At least it's not boring."

Chad chuckled. "Man, I could go for a great big serving of boredom right now."

I understood completely.

Chad turned his gaze into the fissure and raised his voice. "I'm on my way, Corporal."

"It's Lieutenant." Zeke sounded irked.

"Yeah, whatever," Chad said, easing into the fissure. "Don't you recognize humor used as false bravado?"

No response from Zeke. More minutes stumbled by, then we heard Zeke's voice. "I'm in."

"Yay for you," Chad called. Two minutes later he spoke again. "Okay, I guess I'm about halfway, so send the next victim."

"Victim?" Brenda said. "I'm gonna beat the guy so hard his ancestors will scream." She stepped to the opening, paused, and looked at Daniel. "I'll be waiting on the other side for you, kid. Don't make your mama wait."

Daniel grinned. "I'll probably catch up to you. I may even pass you."

"You can try, young man. You can try." Brenda sighed and sidled her way through the gap.

I heard grunting, heavy breathing, then: "Okay, send Daniel."

"Okay, little buddy," I said, "I'll help you into the opening. Now remember—"

"I got it, Tank."

The next thing I knew, the kid had disappeared into the fissure.

Andi chuckled. "This is probably fun for a kid his age."

"That kid's my hero." I pulled Andi to my side. "You're next, kiddo."

"Nope. You're going next," she said. "If you get stuck, I can push you forward or pull you back. It makes more sense for you to go next."

I shook my head. "I might be too big. I could get stuck in there forever. I could be a Tank-cicle."

"That's a cute image, but you're not going to get stuck. I have an idea."

"Am I gonna like it?"

"Not at all. But if you do as I say and it all works out, I'll give you the world's biggest kiss on the other side."

"Now, that's motivation."

"I'm glad you agree." She studied me a moment, then opened her backpack.

We all carried packs for personal items, but we had divvied up items we might need. Zeke had the explosives and trigger devices, Chad carried food and water, and Andi had the medical kit, something Zeke had insisted on bringing.

"What are you looking for?" I asked. She didn't answer.

"Take off your parka." She continued to rifle through her pack, then took out the first aid kit.

"You mean take off my backpack, don't you?"

"That goes without saying." She kept her flashlight

directed on the kit as I dropped my pack. "Ah, here it is. Now, take off your parka."

"Are you trying to freeze me?"

Andi stood with a tube of something in her hand. "No, I'm trying to make sure you get through the fissure. Take off your parka and your shirts. I wanna see bare skin."

"Andi. You've lost your mind."

"Tank, we don't have time to argue. Do it now or I'll strip you down."

If it had been anyone other than Andi, I would have argued longer, but I took off my parka, my insulated shirt, and the thick undershirt I wore. The air in the tunnel bit my skin. "Andi—"

"Hush. Arms up. Do it now."

I did. I reached for the ceiling. She stepped behind me and smeared something on my back.

"What is that?"

"It's sunscreen. Just like the stuff you put on your face before we started this nonsense. Turn around."

I did. She had removed her gloves and worked like a mad woman spreading the cream on my skin. The cold bit my skin like a million invisible piranha.

"This stuff is greasy. It will protect your skin as you rub against the ice. It's slick, meaning you'll get through the ice faster."

"When can I put my parka back on?"

"When you get to the other side. You'll never make it through that space with your parka on. It makes you several inches broader than you already are, and you're plenty broad."

Her hands moved rapidly, applying the goop to my back, my chest, my shoulders, and my arms. I could do nothing but yield. She was the smartest person I knew and that's saying something when you remembered how smart the professor was.

She finished and slipped her gloves back on. "Go, Tank. Go now. It's not going to get any warmer. I'll be right behind you."

I picked up my pack with one hand and my parka and shirts with the other, then slid sideways into the ice fracture. The first three or four steps went just fine, but then the passage narrowed. Soon my bare back was pressed against the ice. Three more steps and both my back and chest were rubbing against frozen surfaces.

"Go, Tank. Push. Keep going."

My arms began to shake and there was no stopping them. The ice felt like a wall of needles. My heart rate rose. My breathing came in ragged breaths. Images of being frozen between two walls of ice played in my brain.

"I think I'm stuck."

Andi had caught up. She put a hand on my shoulder and pushed.

No good.

"I'm wedged in, Andi."

"Lean into it, Tank. Don't give up."

I could tell she stepped back a pace or two. Then came the impact. Andi had thrown a shoulder into my body. I slid forward a couple of inches.

"On the count of three," she said. She counted. I strained. Then another impact. I budged a couple more inches, but I was pretty sure I was just wedging myself in tighter.

"Give me that." Zeke's voice.

I released my parka and shirt.

Another voice. Chad's. "I'll take it . . . he took off

his parka? Why . . . never mind."

"Okay, Big Guy," Zeke said. "This might hurt just a bit. Give me your hand."

I held it up and felt his strong grip on my wrist. My body trembled. This was a lousy way to die.

Then I felt something else on my wrist. Something thick and coarse—a rope.

"On three, give it all you got, Tank."

"I don't think I can. I'm losing it."

"So help me—you give it everything you got or I'm gonna send Brenda in and she doesn't want to come in here again."

"Okay, okay. On three." I leaned toward Zeke and Chad and whoever was behind them. Andi did the best she could to push.

The rope tightened. The loop around my wrist cinched. If I wasn't half frozen, it probably would have hurt.

"Three, two, one..."

The pain was enormous. My arm threatened to pop out of joint, the ice tore at my skin, the narrow passage pushed my ribs closer and closer together—

Then I was free.

The pulling continued, but I was able to keep up with it. A dozen or so side steps later and I was in the room, free of the fissure, but freezing. Everything hurt. Sitting on the floor of the ice room were Zeke, Chad, Brenda, and Daniel. They each held one of the ropes Chad had carried in his pack. All of them looked exhausted.

Chad was the first to speak. He struggled to his feet. "Dude, you're half naked. What have you two been doing over there?"

His snide remark would have bothered me if he

hadn't just rushed to my side to help me get bundled up again.

I hunched over and struggled to draw in one breath after another. The shakes began a moment later.

I'm a big guy. I'm a strong guy. I know how to work through pain. No one makes it far in football without learning to set the aches aside and focus on the next play.

I couldn't set the pain aside. My body ignored my mental pleas. Tremors began in my hands and moved up my arms in seconds, then moved into my chest. Breathing was nearly impossible. Standing was becoming doubtful. Darkness seeped in from the corners of my eyes.

I closed my eyes for a moment, then opened them in time to see blood smeared on the ice near my feet. The ice had torn into the skin of my back and chest.

Swell. Just swell.

I raised my head, then everything dimmed for a moment. I thought I was going under, but the dimness came from Andi pulling my inner shirt over my head. Another thick slip-on shirt followed.

"Stay with me, Tank," she said. "I can't dress you if you pass out. Besides, I promised you a kiss, remember?"

I waited for another snide remark from Chad or even Brenda, but none came. It took three attempts but I managed a weak, shaky, "I remember."

Andi nodded at Zeke. "My pack—"

"I'm on it."

I forced my eyes to the side and saw Zeke rifling through Andi's backpack. I had no idea what he was looking for. My brain was frosting over.

"Give me an arm, Big Guy," Chad said.

I suppose he wanted me to raise my arm, but it didn't want to be lifted. It didn't matter, Chad grabbed my right wrist and raised it chest high. Then he put something on it. The sleeve of my parka. He was putting my coat on. He moved to my left side and grabbed my other arm.

"Leave it open for a sec," Andi said.

Zeke again: "Here. Two on his chest; one on his back.

I looked at Zeke. He was holding a plastic pack, like an ice pack. I didn't want nuthin' to do with an ice pack.

He pulled out a bag, then slapped it against his leg and began squeezing it. He handed it to Andi. "Peel the cover off the tape. The bag will stick to his clothes."

She did and pressed the bag in the center of my chest. It stuck. And it wasn't an ice pack. It was warm. Blessedly, wonderfully warm.

Andi pressed another heat pack on my chest, right over my abs. "Where on his back? High?"

"Yeah," Zeke said. "It will warm his lungs and neck, and that will help warm his blood."

I felt Andi attach the heat pack to my shirt, between my shoulder blades.

Chad buttoned and zipped me up.

"Hold this, Tank." Zeke pressed another heat pack into my hands. "Gotta warm the extremities. If we were on the surface we would warm your arms and legs first, but we're not on the surface and we don't have the equipment to do that. And by the way, that's it for the hot packs."

"You should start feeling better in a minute," Andi

said.

"C-can I s-sit down?" I was feeling weak.

"No," Andi said. "We have to keep you moving. All we can do is warm your body; your body has to warm your blood and circulate it. Okay?"

"Yeah. Okay. If you say so." My voice sounded a little steadier. Breathing was a tad easier.

"Come here." Andi placed a gloved hand on each side of my head and pulled me close. She kissed me. She kissed me long and tender. Her lips seemed to be on fire, but I imagine mine were chunks of ice. "I made a promise. I keep my promises."

Then she did something strange. She nuzzled me, burying her face in my neck. At first I thought she was expressing affection, then I felt her warm breath being forced down my neck. Every few seconds she switched sides. My brained cleared enough for me to figure out what she was doing: She was warming my neck with her breathing.

I had to take sports physiology in college. A lot of athletes did. I didn't excel in it but I did pass—barely. I remembered enough to know that blood travels to the brain by arteries and leaves by veins. She was trying to warm the blood going to and from my noggin. I didn't know if that would work, but I wasn't going to interrupt.

Something grabbed my left leg. I didn't have to look to know Daniel was hanging on as if he could keep me in this life by clinging to me. Then he began rubbing my leg.

Then someone began rubbing my other leg. The friction of the snowsuit against flesh brought a little heat. "Jus' for the record, Cowboy, if you ever tell anyone I did this, I'll deny it, then hunt you down."

"I-I look forward . . . to it."

Chapter 4

A LONG WALK; A LONG TALK

One of the problems in being way deep under the ice and half frozen to death is that it becomes really hard to judge the passing of time. It may have been a half-hour before my friends let go of me and let me walk around on my own. Then again, it may have been half a day. I couldn't tell.

One thing I could tell was that I was feeling a whole lot better. Not perfect, mind you. I was still chilly, hands still felt like five-fingered ice-cubes, and my feet were alternating between numbness and pins-and-needles tingling.

I do know enough time passed for the hot packs to cease being hot. Andi helped me remove them and we stacked them in the corner of the ice room. I hated doing that, but it made no sense to cart them along with us. They would just be useless weight.

While I was warming up my innards, the others chowed down on a few high protein and carb bars.

I used the time to look around the ice room. Zeke had been right, it was about the size of a large bedroom. The passageway we wanted was ceiling high. Going to be a challenge to reach it.

"Why is this room here?" I asked. I shone my light on the walls. The walls and floor of the other tunnel were scalloped. These appeared smooth.

"Don't know," Zeke said. "There's no other way out. We either find a way to get everyone in the tunnel up there or we go back through the fissure.

"Jus' so you know, I ain't going back in the fissure."

I heard Zeke struggle to his feet. "I had a feeling you'd say that. How are you doing?"

"I'm okay. Not at my best, but I shouldn't hang anyone up."

"Good. Then if everyone has had a little rest and food, we should get back to the task at hand."

Chad stared at the opening of the tunnel. "Has anyone else noticed that there's a glow coming from up there? Anyone want to venture a guess as to why?"

"Some kinda light source," I said.

"Astute as that is, Big Guy," Chad said, "It tells us nothing."

"Would wild-eyed guessing help?" Brenda

snapped.

"Easy, girl. I'm just warming the room with my hot air."

"In that case," Brenda said, "keep talkin'."

Chad did. "Zeke, you said you looked down the corridor. Pulled yourself up enough to have a brief look-see."

"Yeah. Just saw a long, descending tunnel."

"Was it glowing then?"

"Now that you mention it, it was."

"Okay." Chad shrugged. "It could be anything, so guessing is a waste of time. Let's go exploring. Frankly, I've had all of this space I want."

No one argued.

"Anyone bring a ladder?" Brenda asked. "I'm not all that good at climbin' ice walls."

"Not a problem." Zeke shone a light around until he found the ropes they used to pull my oversized carcass through the eye of the needle. "Give me some more light over here."

I turned on my light and directed it at the end of the rope Zeke held. In short order, he tied a knot that left a decent size loop, big enough for a large foot.

"And there we have it." Zeke seemed proud. "The handy-dandy bowline knot. In the navy, they make you tie this knot so many times you dream about it."

He moved to the wall with the tunnel near the ceiling. The bottom of the tunnel was at least seven feet above the floor. Not a huge gap, but still a difficult climb.

"Give me a boost, Chad," Zeke said.

"Give you a boost?" Chad usually resisted any idea that didn't first come from him.

"If you're too weak," Zeke said, grinning, "I can

get someone stronger to help me. Like Brenda."

Chad chuckled. "Trying to manipulate me through my pride, eh?"

"Is it working?"

"Yeah, I guess it is."

"I can do it," I offered.

"Not this time, Tank," Zeke said. "You're not a hundred percent, and I got a feeling we're gonna need everything you got later. So you sit this part out."

He was right, but I wasn't going to agree with him. I kept my mouth shut.

Standing beneath the tunnel, Chad put his back to the ice wall and formed a stirrup with his hand. Chad was pretty well put together, so this wasn't going to stress him too much.

Zeke threw the other end of the rope over his shoulder, then put his right foot into Chad's hands. "On three." He counted down and reached for the bottom edge of the tunnel as Chad grunted and lifted. Making it look easy, Zeke disappeared into the opening. A moment later his head appeared and he began pulling the long rope into the tunnel until the bowline loop hovered a foot above the surface we stood on.

"Brenda, you're up."

"Why don't I just give her a boost like I did you?" Chad said.

"Trust me, buddy. I got a plan." Zeke wiggled the rope.

"Sure, sure, make the sister the test subject." Brenda studied the rope and the loop.

Andi joined her. "I think he's gonna call for Daniel next, so he wants you up there with him."

"Makes sense." Brenda put a foot in the loop.

"Okay," Zeke said. "I'm not going to pull you all the way. Just far enough for you to crawl in. Got it?"

"I got it," she said. "Now ask me if I like it."

"We can talk about it when you're up here."

Daniel smiled at her. "You got this, Mom."

"Thanks, baby. You always know what to say." She took a deep breath and gripped the rope. "Haul away, sailor."

Zeke did, lifting Brenda enough for her to crawl in the space with him.

"You ready, Daniel?"

"Yes, sir." He was already at the rope, his foot in the loop. "Looks fun."

Only Daniel could be deep below the ice in a dark, frozen room and think he's at Disneyland.

"Spot him, will you, Tank?"

"You got it." I positioned myself behind Daniel and gave him some advice. "Don't let him pinch your fingers between the ice and the rope. Your mother wouldn't be happy and if your mother ain't happy—"

"Ain't nobody happy," the kid said.

"That's a fact, D-man. That's a fact." I gave his shoulder a squeeze. "Ready?"

"Born ready."

"He's all yours, Zeke."

Daniel began a slow rise. Moments later, the kid was inside the tunnel.

"Andi, the party's up here. Come join us."

"I never get to parties anymore." She took her turn on the rope, rising smoothly and easily. My guess is that Brenda was helping Zeke pull. I was beginning to see his plan.

"You'll be next, Chad," I said. "Zeke is gonna need all the help he can get to tow me high enough to crawl into the tunnel."

"Yeah, I finally figured that out."

A minute later, Chad had joined the others.

Now. Deep breath.

I put my foot in the loop and prayed it would hold. It was one thing to haul up skinny people, but I was going to be a bit more of a challenge.

"We're ready up here, Tank."

I envisioned a long line of my friends ready to start a deadly serious game of tug-o-war.

"Hoist me up."

They did, and I had no problem dragging my fanny into the tunnel even though Zeke was right; I wasn't up to full strength. Just crawling into the tunnel left me winded.

I couldn't help wondering if I was more detriment than asset.

***

The tunnel was fairly wide, spacious enough that we could walk three abreast. We didn't. Instead, we paired off. Zeke had point and Chad walked with him—about a step or two behind.

Chad had lost some of his edginess. He sometimes still worked his mouth, but much of his insulting chatter had disappeared. He also looked like a man with a great deal on his mind.

I suppose that is normal after a soul-flipping change. He kinda reminded me of a man wearing a new suit of clothes and not quite sure where all the pockets were.

Brenda and Daniel followed them. Brenda kept a hand on Daniel's shoulder. To me, she was the bravest of us all. On several missions, Daniel had been crucial to our success and even our survival, but that meant he was in danger, too. No mom could endure seeing such things without being forever scarred.

When we first met, Brenda didn't like the rest of us. Wasn't like the rest of us. And didn't want to be around the rest of us. She was hard as a sixteen-penny nail, quick with a threat, and as Chad found out early on, quick with a punch. She could never take me down, not that I would ever raise a hand to her. I admire that woman more than she knows, more than I can say, but if she ever *did* lay into me, I would carry the bruises for years.

We kept a slow pace forward. Walking on the ice was a challenge and no one wanted to break a leg down here. Adding to that challenge we were using only two of our flashlights.

Andi walked next to me. She kept looking at me, not as a lover, but as a mother. She was worried about me.

"I'm okay," I said. "No need to worry."

She took my hand—glove to glove. The gloves kept my hands warm; Andi kept my heart warm. "Worry is my prerogative. Are you sure you're all right?"

"Yeah. I'm sore. The ice cuts on my chest and back are sticking to my inner shirt. There's some stinging here and there, a few aches, but the good news is I'm still good-looking."

"Sounds like you may have a concussion, too." She followed that with a sweet smile.

"Oh, so that's how it is, eh?"

She squeezed my hand. Gloves or no gloves, it was

a thrill for me.

"I've been meaning to ask you something, Tank." Her tone drifted toward the serious.

"Shoot."

"Before we got distracted with Brenda and her drawing, you were about to say something about Azazel. You said something wasn't right."

"Yeah, I was." I looked at her. "I hate to say this, but I think you're wrong about Azazel." She shot me a glance, not a hard one, but one of those, What are you talkin' about? kinda looks. I can't blame her; Andi is seldom wrong. Seldom.

"I know, I know. You're our research ninja and there's no one better at it, but the fallen angel bit doesn't fit. At least it doesn't fit with the Genesis six fallen angels."

"Um, you know, I'm pretty careful with my research, Tank."

"Yes, you are, and I admire that. You're the perfect blend of beauty and brains."

Brenda huffed. "Oh, gag me."

Chad chimed in with his best Ricky Ricardo accent. "You got some 'splanin' to do, Lucy." He likes old television shows.

"Yeah," Andi said. "Spill it, Tank."

"I'll try," I said. Why not? It would help keep my mind off my physical pains and what lay ahead. "You used the *Book of Enoch* as one of your sources—"

"And you made a point of saying that the *Book of Enoch* is not part of the Bible."

"I did say that—"

"And I reminded you the New Testament quotes from the *Book of Enoch* a couple of times."

"It does." I tried to get my words right, which is

sometimes difficult for me. "That doesn't make the *Book of Enoch* part of the canon."

"Cannon?" Daniel looked over his shoulder at me. "Like a big gun?"

"No, buddy. This canon is different. It's even spelled different." I spelled the word for him using only one *n*. "The word I'm using comes from an old Greek word which meant 'rule,' like a ruler, or a yardstick. Something to measure something else by. Canon includes all sixty-six books in the Bible."

"It's a strange word," Daniel said.

"I guess so," I said, "but my point is, there are reasons why the books in the Bible are in the Bible. Over the centuries, scholars have confirmed those books as genuine. I'm just saying that the Bible has proved itself to be full of truth. It doesn't tell us everything we might wanna know, but it does tell us everything we *need* to know, including a little bit about fallen angels."

"Such as?" Chad said.

"You already heard Andi tell us about the angels in Genesis chapter six. They were angels who left their assigned realm to cohabit with human women."

"And by co-habit you mean—"

"Careful," Brenda said. I didn't think it was possible, but her tone chilled the air. "Young ears over here."

"You know what I'm talking about," I said. "The women gave birth to children who grew to be giants called the Nephilim."

"And," Andi said, "they were all killed in the flood of Noah. Right?"

"Right," I said. "There's lots more to that story, but the part that makes me think Andi's explanation is partly wrong is this: those sinning angels were condemned for what they did and the evil they pushed on the world."

I took a second to recall a Bible verse from the little New Testament book of Jude, verse six. "And the angels which kept not their first estate, but left their own habitation, he hath reserved in everlasting chains under darkness unto the judgment of the great day."

"First estate?" Chad said.

"Many scholars think this refers to the angels of Genesis six. They left their own habitation and because of their actions, God has bound them until the Day of Judgment. There's another verse, 2 Peter 2:4: "For if God did not spare angels when they sinned, but cast them into hell and committed them to pits of darkness, reserved for judgment . . ."

"The two verses are talking about the same thing, but the Peter verse gives us something strange." I let that hang in the cold air for a moment. Truth is, I needed a minute to breathe. My ribs were giving me grief.

"Wait a sec," Brenda said. "There are angels in hell?"

I nodded, but no one saw it, my being at the end of the line and all. "That's the strange thing. Does everyone know that the New Testament is written in old Greek?"

No answer.

"Well, you do now. The Bible was written by over forty different authors on three continents over fifteen hundred years. The Old Testament was written—"

"In Hebrew and Aramaic," Andi interjected.

"Exactly. Mostly Hebrew. The New Testament is in Greek. Anyway, the word that is translated as 'hell' in the English version is the Greek word for *Tartarus*. Tartarus is not hell."

"Now, you've really lost me," Brenda said.

"Remember I said that the Bible doesn't tell us everything we want to know, but it tells us everything we *need* to know? This is one of those cases. The Bible would be too big to read if it told us everything. So, there are parts that leave us with more questions than answers."

"I've heard of Tartarus," Andi said. "The ancient Greeks believed it the worst and darkest place, worse than Sheol—the place of the dead."

"I've sat in on a few Bible studies where the teacher mentioned that," I said.

"Cut to the chase," Chad said. "What are you trying to tell us?"

Andi spoke up before I could. "I think I know where you're going with this. You're saying that Azazel can't be a Genesis six angel because he's not confined to Tartarus. Right?"

"Bingo."

"But he agreed with me when I accused him of it. Why would he do that?"

"He murdered the professor," I said. "It's only a guess, but I'm pretty sure most murderers are liars, too. He doesn't care what we believe."

"Okay, okay, everybody just stop for a moment." Chad turned as we grouped together. "If he's not one of the Genesis six creatures, then what is he?"

"I can't be sure," I said, "but I'll give you my best guess. Either we're in Tartarus with him, and I'm pretty sure that's not the case, or he's an entirely different kinda creature."

Brenda shook her head. "Ain't never heard nothin' like this in Sunday school—when I went."

"Listen," I continued, "I don't have answers, just guesses based on what we've seen and what the Bible said. That ancient document makes one thing clear— we are in a very different kind of battle. Paul wrote: 'For our struggle is not against enemies of flesh and blood, but against the rulers, against the authorities, against the cosmic powers of this present darkness, against the evil spiritual forces in the heavenly places.'"

"Hang on, Bible Boy," Chad said. "We've been thinking aliens and multi-dimensional beings, but you're talking about angels—"

"Not flesh and blood," I said, "but rulers, authorities, cosmic powers, evil spiritual forces—any of that sound familiar?"

"It all sounds familiar," Andi said. "*Too* familiar."

"Think of all we've seen: evil people, monsters, ghost-like creatures, other—what did the professor call them?—other universes in the multiverse. I don't pretend to understand all that, but it sounds like all the stuff we've seen."

"So," Brenda said, "Azazel is one of those cosmic power thingies?"

"My best guess is that he's one of the fallen angels who troubles the nations. That's the best I can come up with."

A moment of silence, then Andi lifted her head. "Does this change our mission?"

"No, we need to do what we set out to do: destroy this place and, God willing, set the bad guys back a few decades."

Zeke, who had remained mum through all of this, finally broke his silence: "Then I say let's do this while we can."

Chapter 5

CHAMBER OF WONDER

Andi moved to one of the ice corridor's walls. "Has anyone else noticed the change in the tunnel?"

"You mean the slope?" Chad said.

"Nope. We've been headed down hill since we started this little trek." She touched the wall with her gloved hand.

I joined her. "Yeah, I see it. The walls are smoother. I noticed that earlier."

"Almost polished." Andi withdrew her hand. "The

49

first tunnel we were in had scalloped surfaces. This one doesn't. I should have picked up on that earlier.

The rest of the team followed Andi's example and examined the walls. All the flashlights were burning, but not for long. After a quick look, the others turned off their lights, leaving only two on so we weren't in pitch black.

"Does that strike anyone as strange?" Andi asked.

Zeke was the only one to answer. "It's the same ice. I would expect some variation, but this seems a bit much. Any ideas?"

More silence, then Chad's voice: "The first part of the tunnel wasn't used much. The builders may have dug it out, but never made use of it. They must have had plans for this area."

"Or," Zeke said, "we might be nearing something important."

Andi agreed.

I didn't offer an opinion. I didn't have a clue why there would be a change.

"It's warmer," Brenda said. "I can feel my nose now."

She was right. Our arctic gear not only kept the cold out, it kept us from noticing temperature changes. I suppose if we walked into a nice warm room, we'd notice that, but not a change of just a few degrees. As little as that might be, it could have had an impact on the ice. I said as much.

Zeke agreed with me, then refocused on the mission. "Let's keep at it. We need to know where this tunnel leads."

"It leads to nuthin' but trouble," Brenda said.

I couldn't argue with that. Apparently, no one else could either.

We continued on in the same order we had been.

We walked another half-mile or so when Chad's voice rolled back to the end of the line. It was one word, a word spoken in a whisper: "Light."

I pushed forward to see. The others must have like the idea because they followed my example. We stood close to each other and gazed down the tunnel. A short distance away was a bluish light, like the light we had seen before reaching the storage area we found when we first entered this underground fortress.

"Ideas?" Chad asked.

Andi huffed. "Like what? We have three choices. One, we go back; two, we sit here until we die of cold or starvation; or three, we keep going."

"I vote we find an escalator we can ride to the surface," Brenda said. "I've had all of this place I want and more."

"Tallyho," Zeke said, and started forward.

The light grew brighter as we approached. I have no idea how there could be light a thousand or so feet below the surface of the ice, but there it was, just like before.

All conversation ceased. We crept forward like an army moving through a field of landmines. The more steps we took, the brighter the light became. Soon we were able to turn off our flashlights.

The tunnel widened and leveled. We were no longer walking downhill. I strained my ears for voices, machine noises, the sound of a demonic Ping Pong game, anything to give me a hint about what we were walking into.

I heard nuthin' but my own ragged breathing.

I inhaled slowly but deeply, then worked my way forward. I needed to be at the front. That's where I could be useful. I was no good at the back of the line.

I wasn't the brains of the operation. I never had been. I've never been the planner or the observant one. For the most part, I've been the muscle. I've managed to use my gift of healing a few times, but most of the time I'm the big guy whose job it is to protect the team. I intend on doing that if I can.

The tunnel emptied into a cave—I mean a *cavern*. It reminded me of Carlsbad Caverns, a place I had seen as a kid, but this one was made of ice instead of stone. The huge place was too big to take in with one glance.

I raised a hand to stop those behind me.

I blinked. Several times. The bright light burned my eyes. I had been in near darkness for a long time and my eyeballs had trouble adjusting. Fortunately, they came around quick enough.

My muscles tightened. My hands curled into fists. My gaze flew around the room looking for what Daniel calls *duch*—the bad guys, more like the bad *things*. We had seen a variety of them during our missions and they all seemed a little different.

I heard a metallic click and glanced to my right. Zeke had stepped to my side; he held a 9mm pistol and he had just racked a round into the chamber. He had removed the glove from his right hand so his finger would fit over the trigger.

"See anything, Big Guy?"

"Not yet. Nuthin' specific."

I struggled to believe what my eyes were showing me. The ceiling rose at least four stories over my head. I felt like a bug under an overturned cereal bowl.

"This place is unbelievable," Andi said.

A quick look told me that everyone had followed me in. So much for hanging back until I checked things out.

The floor was just an open expanse of ice. No furniture anywhere. Although I couldn't tell you why, I had a feeling the space was old—really old.

"This must be part of the complex the Nazis built," Andi said.

"Maybe," I replied. "Or maybe someone else built it and the Nazis just moved in."

"Maybe," Andi agreed.

I stepped toward the center of the room, still straining my ears for any sound that might indicate we weren't alone. Nothing.

Around the edge of the dome I saw other openings. Some large enough to drive a tank through; others that could only accommodate one or two people at a time. All the openings were higher than door height. Well, the usual *human* door height.

I walked toward a side access with the largest opening. There were two such passages. The others followed me. The tall opening gave way to another inverted bowl chamber almost as large as the first one.

I made it three feet inside when something stopped me in my tracks. I stopped so quickly Chad bumped into my back.

"Come on, Tank. Give a guy a little notice. It's not like you're wearing stop lights on your—"

He must have lifted his head. "You gotta be kidding me," he said. "That's... that's..."

Chad doesn't usually lack for words but I couldn't blame him. I looked. I stared. I may have even gawked. I don't stun easily, especially not after what

I've seen recently. The weird and the impossible have become almost commonplace. This view, however, took the cake.

Andi stepped to my left. "Would it be rude of me to say I told you so?"

"Very rude," I said. "But you'd still be right." I leaned forward and placed my hands on my knees. I needed a few extra breaths and a few seconds to pray that I was dreaming. When I straightened, it was still there. I say *it*, but I mean *they*.

"Way cool," Daniel said. He started forward, but a hand grabbed the back of his parka.

"Where do ya think you're going?" There was more statement than question in Brenda's words. "You're staying right here with me and the other sane people."

"But, Mom! It's a flying saucer, just like Andi talked about before we left. A real flying saucer like in the old movies."

Brenda kept hold of Daniel. "I knew I shoulda never let you watch those old sci-fi flicks."

"Okay, then," Chad said, his voice low. "So everyone sees those things, right? It's not just me? I'm not crazy, right?"

"We see them," Andi said, "but you're still probably crazy."

Daniel was getting more amped by the second. "We're gonna go in, right? I mean, they have ramps and everything, so we can just walk in. We gotta go. We gotta. There could be aliens inside."

"They could be cannibals, son."

"Cannibals? Alien cannibals? Aliens can't be cannibals." Daniel was pushing his luck.

"And just how many creatures from outer space

have you met, boy?"

"But, Mom—"

"Let it go, little buddy," I said. "Your mom is right. You gotta keep your emotions in check. Move slowly when you can."

"You're not scared are you, Tank? Are you? Huh?"

"Yep."

I started forward.

"Where are you going?" Zeke asked.

I didn't bother to face him. No telling what he'd read in my eyes. "I'm gonna see what the cannibals from outer space are plannin' for supper."

I didn't have to go alone. Andi was by my side a minute later and she was followed by Chad and Zeke. Zeke still held his weapon.

If you don't repeat this I won't have to deny it, but I love those old sci-fi movies, so a part of me was giddy. Another part of me was about to puke.

A simple ramp ran from the ice floor to the underside of the first craft. No stairway, just a ramp with nonskid material on it. The material looked worn and parts of it were peeling. My guess was that it had not been made for storage in a gigantic ice cavern. But then again, what was?

"Let me go first," I said. "This time, I mean it. Let me go alone. If something bites me, shoots me, hits me with a ray gun or an ice water balloon, I'll let you know."

"What do we do if you come running out screaming?" Chad asked.

"I suggest you move."

After taking a deep breath, I lugged myself up the ramp and into a decent size opening. I fit easily, so I guessed little gray aliens would have no problem.

The saucer or whatever was dark as a tomb inside, so I used my flashlight. The air was stale, but breathable. It smelled like roasted almonds; I have no idea why.

After a quick look-see, I returned to the ramp, descended halfway, then looked for Brenda. I gave her a thumbs up.

She let go of Daniel and he sprinted my way, brushing past the others and running up the ramp. I snagged him with one arm and lifted him. "Okay, dude, here's the deal. I'm gonna let you go in with us, but—"

"Cool!"

I raised a finger on my free hand. "But you gotta make me a promise. You ain't gonna touch nuthin'. Got it? I mean nuthin' but nuthin'. I don't want you accidentally launching us into outer space. Clear?"

"I couldn't do that, Tank. We'd never make it through all the ice. Duh."

"Duh? Really? Duh? You wanna go in, or not?"

"I won't touch anything."

"That's what I wanna hear." I set him on the ramp. "Does your parka still have pockets?"

He gave me a *that's-a-stupid-question* look. "Of course it does."

"Good. Put your hands in the pockets and don't take them out."

The little runt gave me a salute, then buried his gloved hands in his coat. That kid has some kinda sense of humor.

The others stood at the foot of the ramp pretending to be patient. "Let's go. You're gonna need your lights."

***

Beams from flashlights danced around the space, and the bouncing beams reminded me of the *X-Files*. They always had a flashlight scene, and since we were standing inside a flying saucer, the *X-Files* seemed to fit.

I stood by the door—maybe a door is called a *hatch* on a flying saucer. What do I know about such things? I watched the others. I had given my flashlight to Daniel who, for the moment, was the happiest kid on the planet. For a moment, I felt good about it all, but that feeling didn't last long. We were still a thousand or more feet under ice, in danger from a supernatural enemy, and . . . well, I couldn't scrub the image of a crucified professor from my mind. I doubted anyone could. We were doing our best to carry out our mission and trying to distract ourselves from what we had seen, and experienced.

And then there was Brenda's drawing—the drawing that showed all of us but Daniel deader than dead. Something else I wished I could scrub from my brain.

The others looked around in silence for a few minutes, then Chad said what I expected him to say: "Wait a sec. This isn't right."

Andi agreed. "It's not right by a long shot."

"There are three seats near the control panel," Chad continued. "Okay, that makes sense." He turned toward a row of ten seats near the back of the craft. I say *back* because the curved wall was opposite the control panel. "But they're full—"

"Full-sized." Andi finished the sentence for Chad. "Those can hold a full-sized human. So much for little green men . . . or little gray aliens."

"That's because this didn't come off a used spacecraft lot," Zeke said. "Look at the gauges."

"Yeah, I noticed that, too," Chad said. "The gauges are analog. Old technology."

"Analog?" Brenda stepped closer to the panel. If she was impressed with her first glimpse of a flying saucer, she was doing a great job of keeping it secret.

"Yep," Chad said. "These gauges are mechanical, with arms that move over the face of the dial, like an old watch."

"I know what analog means," she snapped. "I may only be a tattoo artist, but I know a few things."

Andi diffused the situation. "I doubt ET could sail the deep regions of space with that kind of low technology."

"Wait," Daniel said. "This *isn't* from outer space?"

"Sorry, kid," Andi said. "I'm a little bummed, too."

Before we began this grand expedition, Andi had told us that many people believed the Nazis set up camp in the Antarctic, found UFOs, and stole some of the alien technology.

"That's all good thinking, people," Zeke said, "but the proof is written on the gauges. The words are German."

"Germans are known for great engineering," Chad added. "Of course, I usually think of cars like Mercedes and Porsche."

"And then there's this." Zeke moved his flashlight to the top of the panel, illuminating a swastika. I had seen it when I first entered. I don't usually anger easily, but that image set my blood to boiling.

Chad slipped into one of the seats and the space filled with light. Even from my position by the door I saw the gauges move. A moment later I heard a smooth hum. Chad was out of the chair in a heartbeat.

"Sorry, sorry." He took several steps back. "I didn't expect that."

The lights dimmed again.

"You should put your hands in your pockets and keep them there," Daniel said.

"We're leaving." Brenda grabbed Daniel by his coat and yanked him toward the hatch.

I stepped aside, then followed them out. At the foot of the ramp, Daniel returned my flashlight. "Here," was all he said.

I took the light. "Sorry it wasn't what you expected, buddy."

"It's okay. It's still pretty cool."

I wasn't sure I could agree. The thing gave me the willies. Everything I saw down here gave me the willies.

The others filed off the ramp.

Zeke shone his light around. "I imagine all these other chambers are storage spaces, but we need to look. We may find a better path or something to help us finish this job and get out of here.

"We should stick together," I said.

"It would go faster if we split up," Chad said.

"No dice." Zeke shook his head. "I'm with Tank on this one. There's strength in numbers."

"I ain't feeling all that strong," Brenda said.

We started for the next chamber.

Chapter 6

CHAMBER OF HORRORS

We moved around the massive chamber investigating the smaller compartments. Some were empty; others had mundane things like basic supplies and even toilet paper. Very old and frozen toilet paper. It made me wonder where the bathrooms were located.

Andi had grown talkative—a sign she was getting nervous. "Zeke, what do you think the Nazis did with the flying saucers?"

"My guess is that you might be right and they engineered their own saucers from one they found here or someplace else. They were working on rockets—the V1 and the V2. The V2s did a lot of damage to London. Maybe the saucer was going to be the next wave of tech to prosecute the war."

"So the seats in the back of the craft were for soldiers?" she asked.

"Maybe. Or maybe they were used to ferry around bigwigs. Allied bombers and fighter jets described some pretty strange aircraft they called *foo fighters*. Maybe those things were what they were seeing." He sighed. "I'm just spit-balling here. Of course, there are some people who believe that several Nazi leaders escaped to South America. Some say that Hitler made it out, too. I suppose having your own flying saucer might make escape easier."

"I thought Hitler killed himself," Chad said.

"That's what most believe, but others hold a different opinion. For all we know, he came here. We do know there was a lot of planning to restart the war from South America. Those guys didn't give up easily."

"I wanna know how they got those things out of here and into the air," Chad said.

"That's what we're looking for," Zeke said. "They had to fly those things in, so I assume they must have been able to fly those things out."

"Which would explain the UFO sightings in Antarctica," Andi said.

Zeke nodded. "Exactly."

He led us into yet another chamber. This one was larger than most and held a machine shop. That made sense. More and more I felt like we were strolling through a haunted factory—a frozen, haunted factory.

I was bringing up the rear, not because I'm lazy or slow, but because it was the place for me to be, what Zeke called a "tactical position." I was the last to enter each of the manmade ice caves.

The team filed through the opening. I would be the last to enter, but before I made it inside, I heard a scream, maybe two or three screams (one sounded like Chad) that made me hold up. As I did, dim figures came charging toward me, their flashlights cutting through the darkness like light sabers.

Brenda shot past me carrying a package. It took a second for my startled brain to realize that Daniel was the package.

"*Duch, duch,*" Daniel screamed.

Behind them came Chad, then Andi. Zeke was the last to hot-foot it out of the space.

"Run, Tank!"

I held my ground and steeled myself to face whatever was attacking them. I raised my light, partly to see, partly to blind the thing heading my way.

Nothing came.

I took two steps forward and listened. No footsteps. No growling. No snarling. No breathing. Nuthin'. Still, I didn't relax. *Something* had sent the others sprinting out of the area.

The reaction of the others told me I should back out the way I came. That would make sense, but I don't always do the sensible thing.

I scanned the room with my flashlight, the beam reflecting off the ice walls and ceiling. Ten feet in, I saw a rectangular box on a stand. Moving my beam left to right I saw other rectangular boxes. The more I looked, the more boxes I saw. I say *boxes* because that was my first impression. It took me a few moments to realize that each box reflected more light than it should have if it was made of wood or the like.

I figured the size of each box to be about six, maybe seven feet long, and best I could tell, they were less than three free feet wide. They sorta reminded me of . . . coffins.

I've been cold since we were lowered through the ice shaft, but this realization put an extra measure of chill in my marrow. They were the right size and shape to be coffins. Yep, backing out made the most sense.

So I moved forward.

I approached the first row of boxes. I'm only guessing, but there must have been close to a hundred of them in this room, all lined up neat and orderly. For some reason, I found that even more unsettling.

When I got within touchin' distance I directed my light to the box's lid.

Man, I wish I hadn't done that.

The lid was glass or some kinda, thick, clear plastic. I didn't feel the need to touch it to find out. I'd just have to learn to live without that answer.

My beam fell on something dark gray. Then I saw a leather strap, like a belt, but across the body. Only a few seconds had to pass for me to realize I was looking at the body of a man in a Nazi uniform. Maybe Gestapo. Maybe some other branch of the Nazi military. I don't know about such things. Never wanted to know such things.

I ran my light over the dead dude's torso. Definitely a Nazi uniform.

It had to be done. I was in this far, I might as well

go all the way: I shone my light on the man's face.

He was looking at me. His skin was gray and pulled tightly over his skull. I could see his teeth. He looked like he had grimaced, as if my light hurt his unseeing eyes.

I don't remember much of the history I learned in school, but I know World War II ended in the mid '40s. If this guy lived back then, he was really old. He looked it. He looked like he had been dead a long—

I heard something. A creak. Like a hinge on the door in an old Hollywood ghost movie. I scanned the area, but saw nothing.

I heard it again, but this time from a slightly different direction. Still I saw nothing. My nerves were getting to me. No wonder the others had run off.

Time to take a few deep breaths. My nose squeaked as I inhaled. Anyplace other than a frozen morgue and that would have been funny.

There was no need, best I could tell, to look in all the coffins. One scarecrow Nazi was enough for me. I looked at my friend in the box one last time.

He looked back at me, and his eyes seemed narrower than they had a moment ago.

He blinked.

The lid swung up, opening with the sound of rushing air.

I backed away as another lid screeched and opened.

It was reflex, not courage, that made me scan the room with my light again. All the lids were open. Fifty, a hundred, I-don't-know-how-many lids were open and the people inside were rising.

And they were all looking at me.

I would like you to think I was calm, brave, and reasonable; that I evaluated the situation and made a rational decision.

I wasn't. I didn't.

I screamed like a little girl.

And I ran.

The distance from where I stood to the opening was just a few strides, but it seemed closer to a mile. With every step I took, I could imagine—I could feel—a gray, bony hand reaching for the back of my parka.

I plunged through the opening with one thought on my mind and one word in my mouth.

"RUN."

My brain still functioned enough for me to recognize Chad's voice. "If Tank is running, then I'm running too."

I tried to slow enough to let the others get in front of me. A nice idea, but I slipped and hit the ice. I was already sore beyond words from being stuck in a jagged ice opening and this wasn't going to help. Pain rifled up my hip and into my spine. My shoulder complained, too. I had also bounced my head off the ice, hard enough to knock out most men, but I was too scared to pass out.

"Tank!" Andi was beside me in a second. "Are you hurt?"

"Go. Run. Now. Go. Go. Go."

She wouldn't leave until I was on my feet again. Man, I love that girl.

"This way." Zeke stood by the one opening we hadn't entered. He was pointing his light at himself so we could see where he was. "Let's go. Move it, people. Move it!"

We moved it. I hoped—I more than hoped—I prayed that the opening led to someplace other than another storage area where they kept more people-sicles. We had reasoned that the flying saucers had to be trucked or even flown into this place. How else could they be stored here? Sure enough, the opening didn't lead to another side chamber, but to a wide ice tunnel.

As we plunged into the passageway, I felt a bit like Jonah being swallowed by the great fish.

The tunnel was long—so long we couldn't see the end. I guessed we had run a quarter mile before we slowed. Brenda, Daniel, and Andi were huffing and puffing. To be honest, so was I, and I was supposed to be in great shape.

Zeke slowed, then stopped, letting us pass him. When I reached him, he was shining his light forward, looking ahead in the tunnel. I stopped and did the same.

"Those things have been dead too long to put up much of a chase," he said.

"Don't bet your paycheck on that, Zeke. What you say might be logical, but there ain't nothing logical about the things we've seen."

The others came back to join us. "There are certain laws of physics," Chad began. He looked back the way we had come and didn't finish. Coming down the tunnel was a mob of monsters in Nazi uniforms. Chad sighed. "I hate being wrong."

"They're picking up speed," Andi said. "That's not humanly possible."

"They're not human," I said. "We're the only humans down here."

"I could shoot a couple of them," Zeke said, "but

I don't have enough bullets for all them."

"They're already dead," I pointed out. "Bullets aren't going to be much help."

"So, we run," Zeke said.

"We run," I said.

We ran.

A few minutes later, Zeke slowed. "Keep going," he told me. "Don't stop. Don't stop for anything."

I noticed he had removed his pack.

I slowed to his pace. "You hurt?"

"No. Keep the others going. I'll join you in a moment."

"What are you thinking—"

He seized the front of my parka with his left hand and yanked me forward until we were nose to nose. "Tank, stop arguing. Do as I say." He pushed me back with surprising strength.

I hesitated.

"Here, take this." He handed me his backpack. It was then I realized he held something in his hand.

One of the explosive charges.

"Zeke—"

"So, help me, Tank, I'm gonna slap you so hard your head will spin on your shoulders. Now go take care of the others. You're eating up my escape time."

I don't respond well to threats, but for some reason, his worked nicely. I was on the move.

It didn't take long for me to catch the others. They were running out of juice. Too much distance, too much cold, too much fear.

"Where's . . . Zeke?" Andi asked, trying to catch her breath.

"He said he'd catch up."

"How is that possible? We can't leave him—"

A masculine voice rolled down the corridor behind us. "Down. Down. Duck and cover. Look away."

Zeke. And he sounded serious. I grabbed Andi and pushed her to the ice, covering her with my body. I knew what was coming, but the others didn't.

Brenda didn't hesitate. She and Daniel were on the ice, their backs to the corridor, Brenda placing her body between Daniel and whatever was coming. "Oh God," she said, "oh sweet, loving God." I'm not sure, but I think that might have been her first prayer.

"What is going on?" Chad remained on his feet.

But not for long. Zeke executed a perfect crackback tackle and they landed hard. I heard an "Oof" from Chad.

No more time for words or thoughts. The sound jabbed my ears, and a gust of wind that would have swamped a good size ship rolled over us. The air was warm and stank of something burning. I hoped I was inhaling stuff from the explosion and not the burned bits of Nazi zombies.

"Ow, my ears," Chad said. "Ow, my back. Ow, my everything."

He was right. My bones seemed to vibrate like a tuning fork, my innards jiggle like Jell-O, and someone was beating a gong in my head.

"I think you can get off me now, Big Guy." Andi's voice sounded distant. "I can't breathe."

"Oh, sorry." I rolled off her and sat up. Just as I expected, more pain. I struggled to my feet and saw a light skimming the top of the ice. My flashlight. I retrieved it and pointed the beam down the corridor.

There wasn't much of a corridor anymore. It looked like an avalanche had happened fifty feet behind us. Nothing was going to be coming or going up that passageway anytime soon.

"What is the matter with you, Zeke?" Chad said. "Did you have to hit me so hard?"

"Sorry. I thought a smart man like you would have listened and got down."

"That's it. Physical attack and now you question my intelligence. I'm gonna kick you to the curb."

Zeke rose and swayed on his feet a moment. "Really? When you gonna do that?"

Chad paused for a moment. "I don't know. Maybe next month. You got any time then?"

"I'll check my calendar." Zeke helped Chad up.

"Brenda? Daniel?" I said. "You guys okay?"

Daniel spoke first. "My ears hurt, but I'm good. Mom?"

"I don't wanna talk about it." Brenda pushed herself upright. "That's it, guys. I'm done with all this. I'm planning a career in fast food."

I pulled Brenda and Daniel close and hugged them. I kissed Brenda on the head. She hates it when I do that.

"Get off me, you giant side of beef."

I kissed her on the head again. She didn't resist.

"How much of that stuff did you use?" I asked Zeke.

"Beats me. I just grabbed one of the charges. It might have been one of the big ones."

"Might have?" Chad said. "Might have been one of the big ones? Ya think?"

"Hey, I was a little rushed."

We sat for a minute in silence, each of us letting the realization sink in—we were lucky—or blessed— to be alive.

"Now what?" Brenda asked.

"We finish what we came to do," I said. That's when I felt something smack the bottom of my boot.

I wasn't the only one.

"What was that?" Andi jumped back.

I shone my light on the ice at her feet and wished I hadn't. Something was looking at us through the ice. Something with sharp teeth and a bad disposition.

Chapter 7

A SLIPPERY BRIDGE TO NOWHERE

I'm just gonna say it: Since I became part of this team I've seen too many things with sharp teeth. I've seen a bunch of other creepy things too, but the things with teeth creep me out the most.

"What is that?" Chad's voice had gone up an octave.

"It's ugly, is what it is," Brenda said and took a couple of steps back, keeping Daniel in tow.

I stepped back myself. Something hit the ice beneath my boot—again. A couple of the others jumped and looked down. It appears we each had our own ice eel. I don't know if was really an eel or not, but, best I could tell, it was shaped like an eel, and had eely eyes that glowed red as they moved through the ice.

"Not possible," Chad said. "The ice down here is as hard as concrete. Nothing could move through the ice like that. I mean, it's like they're swimming through solid ice. It—it's *impossible*."

My brain was having trouble accepting what my eyes were telling me. Chad was right, eels—even ugly as sin impossible eels like these—couldn't move through solid ice. Not only that, they had some way of making the ice around them clear. Another impossibility that was happening right before our eyes.

A head popped through the ice three feet in front of Chad. He let loose a shout that echoed through what remained of the corridor.

The eel thing thrashed and wiggled and in less than a handful of seconds it was writhing on the surface of the ice. The thing was gray, milky white, and about three times thicker and longer than any eel had a right to be. Steam rose from its body as if it had lava for blood. Maybe that's how they got around in the ice. Maybe. Maybe not.

We heard a bang, sharp, and ear-pounding. The eel scooted backward a couple of feet, a hole in its head. The wiggling stopped.

Zeke stood to the side, his pistol in hand. I waited for someone to make a witty remark, but no words came.

Then another eel emerged. Again, I looked at my feet and I could see through the top layers of ice, something I couldn't do before. A swarm, or a school, or whatever you call a group of massive ice eels swam just below my feet.

"It might be wise to leave." I tried to sound calm, but I'm pretty sure my voice cracked.

"Take the lead, Tank."

Zeke kept his pistol drawn and his hand extended. I got the unspoken message: he wanted to bring up the rear so he could blast any eel that showed its really, *really* ugly head.

"Let's go, guys." I started walking through the corridor at a brisk pace. Chad stayed at the rear and shouted "Clear" every dozen steps or so. He was on the lookout for more eels. I did the same from the front. I feared they would open a hole and we'd all drop in and become eel chow.

I heard more shots fired and prayed that Zeke was all right. We needed him. The good news was I didn't hear any screams.

I kept us moving quickly, but not recklessly. Panic would do us no good. As long as Chad was shouting "Clear," I was content to keep our speed reasonable for the conditions. Falling and breaking a leg down here could be a real problem.

After a few minutes, I slowed to a stop. The sound of heavy breathing behind me told me the others were about spent. Daniel was young, but he was more of a sit-and-play-video-games kinda kid, not a run-outside- and-play kinda of child.

I directed my flashlight beam at the ice, looking for uglies. I saw none. The others did the same. I took a moment to catch my breath, then suggested that Andi, Brenda, and Daniel turn off their lights. At the rate we are going, we would run out of juice soon.

"Let's change batteries," I said. "Doesn't make

much sense to wait until things go dark. We can always swap out again if need be."

No one argued. Most didn't have the wind in them for- it. Chad, was in pretty good shape, so he recovered the fastest. He turned his light back down the corridor. "Come on, Zeke."

He sounded worried and I said so.

"Of course, I'm worried. I can't see him and he has the only gun."

"You're all heart," Andi said.

"I'm nothing if not practical."

"Whatever." Andi bent, supporting herself with her hands on her knees. "Man, I wish I was a smoker so I could give it up."

"No, you don't," Brenda said. She had been the only smoker in our group. She kicked the habit sometime back, but it wasn't easy. I'm sure she did it for Daniel's sake, not ours or hers.

Chad kept flicking his light over the ice. "I don't see anything. Maybe we outran them."

"Maybe," I said.

"Come on, Tank. I'm supposed to be the brains— well, me and Andi—and you're supposed to be the optimist. I could use a little optimism."

So could I, but I didn't say so.

The sound of footfalls echoed in the tunnel. Zeke was safe and making his way to us.

"Staying behind to give us a chance to run was a brave thing to do," Andi said. "Thanks."

Zeke grinned. "I thought about giving the gun to Chad, but I was afraid he'd shoot me in the back."

Chad didn't look hurt, he just smirked. "I didn't know you navy guys had such a sense of humor."

"Only when it comes at someone else's expense."

Zeke moved to the front and looked at me. "We have to keep going. I think those things will be here soon. They're quick, but they can't catch a running person."

"Maybe they gave up," Chad said.

"I wish, but I think they have a plan."

"Yeah," Brenda said. "To eat us."

Zeke shook his head. "I don't think so. I think they're herding us."

"Whoa, back up." I held up a hand. "You mean they're driving us like cattle?"

"Yep. They could have had me for lunch back there, but they didn't do what I expected. They showed intelligence, or they're being guided by someone intelligent. They popped up through the ice, but always stayed between me and the collapsed tunnel. I got the feeling they were trying to get me to move on."

"Maybe we're on their breeding ground—breeding ice," Andi said. "Whatever."

"Possible, but I doubt it. Someone wants us to keep going, and since we can only move in one direction, we'll have to go that way."

I left the front and took my place at the rear. Andi joined me. We all started following the path again.

A hundred or so steps along, Andi said, "I hope Zeke is wrong." She took my hand. Again I wished we could hold hands without the gloves. "If he's right, it means Azazel hasn't forgotten us."

"I never thought he had." I kept my voice low. "He has to know we can't get out going back the way we came."

"I wouldn't be surprised if he caused the ice to shift and cut off our escape route."

"You know I'm not a betting man, but if I was, I'd

drop money on that. It happened at just the right time to trap us."

"He's toying with us," she said. "I wondered why he didn't come after us and finish us off like—" She swallowed hard. "You know."

I thought of the professor, then my mind filled with the image of Andi hanging on a cross. The horror of that moment felt as if someone jabbed my brain with a cattle prod. I stuffed the image away.

"If Azazel truly is a fallen angel, Genesis six or not, he is an eternal being. He has all the time in the world. He can play with us until our provisions run out and we become part of the ice landscape."

"He'd probably enjoy that."

"No doubt." I checked the ice behind us. No ice eels. Then another horrible thought popped into my head. I had been checking the ice floor because that's where we first saw the critters, but those things could just as easily be in the ice walls or the ceiling. I checked those, too. I could just imagine a few dozen ice eels dropping on our heads from above.

A movement in the shadows caught my attention. One of the eels was "swimming" through the ice wall of the tunnel. I checked the other wall. Several more were there. I could also see a school of them gliding through the ice ceiling. Great. Jus' great.

When we first saw them, they were agitated and aggressive. Now they seemed calm. Yep, Zeke was right—they were herding us.

I wanted to try something. "Keep walking," I said to Andi. "I'm gonna stop for a moment."

"Why?"

"I'll tell you in a sec." I let go of her hand and came to a halt. Andi kept going, just as I asked.

I kept an eye on the eels and sure enough, some of them stopped when I did. One of the group to my right turned its head so the red eye on the side of its head stared directly at me. The longer I waited, the more agitated it became.

Then his head burst through the wall and he screeched. I got on my horse and fell into line. Message received, loud and clear.

When I caught up to Andi I nodded. "Yep. Herding us."

"Lovely." No one had to tell me that was sarcasm.

We marched on. As long as we were moving, the ice-eels were happy.

We didn't share their joy.

***

Time passed slowly. My chest and back still hurt a good bit, but now my legs were aching and I was having trouble feeling my feet. Not a good sign. When you're in a frigid environment, losing sensation in your extremities is the first sign that things are about to go horribly wrong.

Then the tunnel disappeared as we entered yet another cavern, one large enough to hold two or three football fields. The ceiling was so high we could barely see it.

Then a realization dawned on me. There was light in this place. I don't know where it came from, but we could see without our flashlights. That was good.

What was bad was what we were allowed to see. A great chasm lay before us. A monster hole hundreds of yards wide and long. Across it was a simple bridge made of ice. I saw no other structure. I wanted to see I-beams, steel cable, and sturdy railings, but all I saw was a frozen footpath, spanning a greater distance than should be possible.

I moved closer to the bridge and looked over the edge of the ledge we stood on. It might have been wise to resist that urge. The ledge was really a cliff, and below—I mean hundreds of feet below—was a lake. Not a frozen lake, but a moving lake of water. I once said I couldn't believe that lakes were buried under the ice, but now I knew better.

"You know," Andi said. "I used to like surprises. I loved weird stuff like this. Now, not so much."

We had reached a dead end, and that gave me good reason to be concerned about our herders. When I looked back at the tunnel we had exited, I saw twenty or thirty eel heads sticking out of the walls.

We couldn't go back there.

"They want us to cross the bridge," I said.

"Ha! Ain't gonna happen, Big Guy," Chad said. "I'll take my chances with them before I'll take a leap into that frigid water."

"It's not frigid," Zeke said. "Lakes like that are formed when bedrock is warmed by magma. It melts the ice and lakes and underground rivers form. Of course, the water only has to be a few degrees above freezing—"

"Really, guys," Brenda said. "You think this is a good time for a science lesson?"

Neither man responded. What could they say?

"Do you think they'll let us cross one at a time?" I asked.

"I doubt it," Zeke said. "It's pretty narrow, so we'll have to go single file. There are no handrails, so stay in the middle of the bridge. Don't look down. Keep your eyes on the bridge. Maintain an even pace." He took a deep breath. "I'll go first."

He didn't wait for a response. He centered his backpack and started to cross. Several times I saw his feet slip and my stomach dropped each time I saw it. The bridge was smooth and slippery.

"It's like walking on oil." Zeke's voice was solid, calm, but I could hear a fair bit of hesitation.

"If *he's* having trouble with this," Andi said, "then how can we cross?"

"We don't have a choice," I said. "We do this."

"I don't think I can." Brenda's voice shook and she was unshakable.

The ground shuddered.

"Great," Chad said. "Just what we need—an earthquake."

"I gotta get Daniel across." Brenda reached for her son.

"No, Mom, you can't carry me. I'll pull you over. You go first."

"I ain't leaving you. Now come here."

"No, you don't." Chad stepped between them. "Come here, kid. You and me, buddy. You and me."

Daniel and Chad had a special relationship. At times, they could read each other's minds. I've seen them carry on a conversation when they were miles apart. But that was when Chad was doing his bilocating stuff, his soul projection or whatever it was. I never fully understood it, but he could travel outside his body and see things others couldn't, but he had learned it could open doors to some very nasty things. It was one reason we were in this fix.

"What do you think you're doing?" Brenda clinched her fists and glared at Chad. Those two had gotten into it before. We didn't need that now.

Chad surprised me. He extended a hand and touched the side of Brenda's head. It was a loving touch. A knowing touch.

"I'm stronger. I can do this. Trust me."

"But—"

"You follow after me—"

Daniel squealed. One of the ice eels had popped through the ice and took a shot at biting the boy. Fortunately, Daniel can be quick, and so can I. I introduced the eel to the toe of my boot, kicking it into the abyss.

"Okay, you win." Brenda was on the verge of tears—something else I'd never seen, but I certainly understood. "Take him. Go. But if you drop him . . . *please* don't drop him."

"Let's go, kid." Chad hoisted Daniel in his arms. He held Daniel in front, keeping his backpack on his back. "Wrap your legs around my waist and your arms around my neck."

Daniel did.

"Good. Now close your eyes and bury your face. No looking around. Got it?"

"Got it."

"Your mom will be right behind us."

Brenda nodded. "You bet I will."

"Okay." Chad took several deep breaths. "Rock and roll."

I kept looking for another jumping jack ice eel, but I had to watch Chad, Daniel, and Brenda cross. I've felt more than my share of fear in my life, but this moment threatened to undo me.

"Go," I whispered. "Go, go, go."

They went.

I could hear Chad talking to Daniel, but I had no idea what he said. Maybe he was boring him with some story from his life.

Daniel didn't move. Chad had told him no looking and Daniel didn't look, didn't budge. Didn't shift his weight. The boy knew how to be still.

Brenda walked close behind, but not too close. At first I thought she was having trouble and moving slower, then it hit me. She was staying out of arms reach. If she slipped she would, like anyone, reach for support and Chad was the only support nearby—Chad and Daniel. If she slipped, she meant to go down alone.

They reached the other side in less time than Zeke. Good for them. Chad set Daniel down, and Brenda picked him up again. A moment later she set Daniel down and grabbed Chad in a hug.

Whaddya know. Miracles still existed.

"Um, Tank." Andi's voice carried a truckload of fear. "We better get going."

She looked back to the tunnel. Eels—by the dozen—poured from the walls and squirmed our way. Others erupted from the ice floor.

Andi was right. Time to go.

She took the lead and I followed a few feet behind. I followed Zeke's instruction and kept my eyes glued to the narrow path. I wished I didn't have to. Eels were tunneling through the bridge, turning white ice clear as if they wanted us to watch. I didn't have to be an engineer to know that burrowing through the ice would weaken the bridge.

Andi noticed the same terror and picked up the pace. I tried to keep up, but she was far more coordinated than me.

An eel broke out of the ice between us. I tried to slow my pace and lost my footing. I fell. Face first. On to the bridge. My head in general, my nose in particular, bounced off the ice. Something warm ran down my face.

I heard a hiss. I raised my eyes and saw the hideous mug of the eel. He wiggled, pulling himself from his hole. I tried to push myself up, but the creature was faster at its task than I was at mine. An image of that thing latched on to my face ran through my brain.

Then a shadow. Then a boot, then an angry scream from a lovely woman. Andi had turned around, backtracked a few steps, and at great risk of sending herself off the edge, kicked the crap out of the eel.

I got a glimpse of it spinning through the air.

"Can you get up?" she asked.

"I can't stay here." I pushed to my hands and knees, then carefully rose to my feet.

"Follow me."

"Anywhere, darlin'. I'll follow you anywhere."

Step after step, short stride after short stride, we finally made to the other ledge. We celebrated with a short group hug.

"Okay," Chad said. "What say we never do anything like that again."

That was easy to agree to.

I swiped at my nose to remove the blood, but it was frozen. I peeled it off instead.

We stood at the mouth of a tunnel that looked as if it had once been part of the tunnel we left behind. No way to tell and it didn't much matter. It was the only way open to us.

We searched the floor, the walls, and the ceiling for eels and saw none—yet.

Zeke pulled on his backpack. I wondered when he had taken it off.

We marched off again, too tired to talk, too frightened to stand still. The herding had worked. We had crossed the bridge and lived.

Of course, living might not be such a benefit. There might be more pain ahead.

The light that lit the gigantic cavern was in this tunnel, too. Could have used this light earlier. I tried not to think about what would happen next, if we would succeed in bringin' this place down, or if Brenda's picture really meant we were all going to die. Instead I focused on moving one numb foot in front of the other.

"Heads up," Zeke said, stopping our little train.

I raised my head and looked at the path before us. Once again, we were not alone. A man stood alone a short distance off. He wasn't a giant like Azazel. That was good. He wasn't a living corpse in a Nazi uniform. That was good too. He was far enough away that I couldn't make out his face in the dim light, but he seemed familiar.

"Welcome. Welcome. My, what an adventure you have had."

I knew that voice, the pattern of speaking.

The man approached like he was an old friend.

Then I recognized him and my gut twisted into a knot.

Chapter 8

MY DEAR, DEAR ENEMY

Ambrosi Giacomo looked a lot like the last time I'd seen him: handsome, well dressed, slick black hair, and big smile. Except last time I saw him he was dead, really and truly dead. He also had a hole in his neck. A big, gory, ugly hole. I remember it because the team put it there.

He smiled. It was a broad smile with a hint of sincerity and an extra measure of menace. "It is so good to have company. We don't get many guests down here."

"Oh, I don't know," Chad said. "We've seen some of your other guests. I can't say you have good taste in friends."

Ambrosi's smile evaporated. I doubt I need to tell anyone this, but though Ambrosi looks good on the outside, he's nothing but death and decay on the inside. He was soulless, ruthless, meaner than a kennel full of rabid dogs. He was also what the Bible called the antichrist. I should never have healed him.

But I did.

You read right. It wasn't that long ago. We were in China hunting for a guy the professor had turned us onto. That guy was Ambrosi and before all was said and done, we all were circling the drain of death. Brenda took a bullet in the shoulder. Chad was doing his bilocating thing, slipping from this world into a spiritual one, and not the healthy kind spiritual. Think, demons and evil spirits and things we don't have names for. Ambrosi orchestrated the attack. The lives of hundreds of tourists were at stake. There was panic. There was shooting. There were children in danger. Chad saved one, but couldn't keep the kid from running off as soon as he could.

When Chad works his bilocating talent, he becomes invisible to us, but not to the beasties at Ambrosi's command. And not to Ambrosi, I might add.

In the end, Chad coordinated all our skills and talents and attacked Ambrosi.

We killed him deader than dead. And that brings us back to my healing him—giving him his life back. I can't live with the knowledge that I killed someone. Not directly. Not intentionally. The team still hasn't forgiven me.

I'm not sure I've forgiven myself.

Ambrosi stepped close to Chad, getting almost nose to nose. He seemed to have no fear of us or anyone else. This was his domain.

The evil grin split his face again. "There's something different about youuuuu. You're not the same Chad Thornton I've come to know and loathe."

Chad had confessed Christ down here. I'm convinced his messing around between worlds opened his head up to all kinds of evil. The evil ones were tracking us through Chad and Chad had no idea. He had been reluctant to come clean, fearing he'd lose his powers. But oh, what he'd gained . . .

Chad took a step back and grinned. "Dude, when was the last time you brushed your teeth? You got a serious case of mouth stench."

"You did it, didn't you?" Shaking his head, Ambrosi retreated a step. "You went religious. What a waste. You were supposed to be the smart one. And you were so useful to us."

Chad lowered his head for a moment as if he was ashamed of his confession. Then he lifted his head again. "I am the smart one," he said, "and I think Tank has been right all along. Yeah, I prayed and my prayer was answered, so I'm feeling pretty good about all of that."

Several unexpected and nice thoughts about Chad rose in my head. Who knew?

Ambrosi turned to me. "Mr. Bjorn Christensen, forgive me, but I've not thanked you for all the good you did for me. I owe you my life. Thank you."

"It's just Tank, and if you're really feeling grateful, you can let my team leave."

"Oh, I wish I could, but circumstances are what

they are. You and your friends used to be annoyances. Speed bumps in the Gate's plans. Nothing more. We tolerated you more than we should have because you were just a band of people with gifts you hadn't mastered, people with loads of courage and not much sense."

"But things are different now. So no, sir, I won't let them go. I won't let *you* go."

"Some gratitude," I said. "After I saved your life and all."

"You know, Tank," Ambrosi continued, "I've toyed with the idea of killing all your friends in front of you to see how many you can bring back to life. What an experiment! Will your gift fail like it has before? What would that be like? Seeing your companions mauled on the ice and you unable to help them. Who knows, I might let you live just so I can watch you writhe in the torment of your failure."

"You leave him alone." Daniel pulled free of Brenda's grasp and took three steps forward.

Ambrosi backpedaled as if Daniel was a pit bull who had just chewed through his leash.

"Daniel!" Brenda grabbed him by his backpack and pulled him behind the others.

"You brat," Ambrosi said. "You worthless little worm. You accident of nature. You—"

That's when I planted my fist on the side of his head. I'm sure it was unwise, but man, did it feel good. Even as I did it, I knew there'd be a price to pay, but no one calls Daniel names in my presence. No one.

"Um, Tank—" Chad began.

Here it came. One more thing I shouldn't have done. One more stupid choice on my part, and Chad couldn't overlook an opportunity to throw it in my face.

"That was beautiful," Chad said, grinning. "That was a work of art. My man, you rock."

Before I had time to process what I was feeling and hearing, my feet left the ice. I was slammed and pinned to the ceiling. Air left my lungs. There was pressure on all sides of me. I was being squeezed to death.

"Let him go." Andi shouted. "He saved your miserable life."

Ambrosi laughed. He was having fun.

Andi launched herself at him and got a powerful backhand to the side of her face, dropping her like a bag of laundry.

I roared. Fought. Tried to turn over so I could push against the ceiling—maybe push myself close enough to grab the guy who just slapped my girl.

Nothing.

I saw Andi try to rise, but she couldn't manage it. Chad rushed to her side, but was sent skidding over the ice back down the corridor—the corridor with the eels. They had made it to this side.

I heard him scream. Such a horrible scream, accompanied by visions of Chad writhing on bloody ice, eels latched to him like leeches to the bare legs of a swimmer.

From my elevated vantage point, I saw him stagger out of the tunnel a moment later. Three tenacious eels were gnawing on his legs. Zeke bounded to him, flashlight in hand, and beat the eels until their spines broke. Their jaws snapped open, releasing Chad. Chad dropped to his hands and knees.

"This isn't China," Ambrosi said. "I will not be

stopped so easily. I've had plenty of time to consider what I was going to do to each of you."

As my vision darkened with rage, I fell, landing hard on the ice.

"I've been waiting for this moment," Ambrosi went on. "Planning your deaths. Not just your deaths, but death at my hands." Ambrosi took a step closer to the broken huddle we had become.

Andi was still on the floor, but conscious. I glanced at Chad who had his eyes closed, his lids pressed together like the jaws of a vice.

His mouth moved. It was easy to guess what he was doing. He was trying to work his gift, to shift his soul into the space between our world and the spiritual, multi-dimensional realm.

"It's not working anymore," Chad said, his voice breaking. "I've lost it. I'm powerless. I'm . . . normal."

"Pity," Ambrosi said. "Not that it matters. I am as prepared for you on that plane of existence as I am on this one."

"For the love of all that is holy," Chad said, opening his eyes. "Just kill us and be done with it. Listening to you prattle on is torture."

"I have no love for the holy, and torture is what I have on my mind." He crossed his arms as if he was a man with no worries. "Haven't you wondered why you got away from Azazel so easily?" He sounded like a college professor talking to dimwitted students. "He wanted to kill each of you, but I talked him into resisting that impulse. Of course, I had to give him something for his efforts, so I gave him your professor. I was fine with that. What I really wanted was you . . . in front of me . . . dying a long, slow death. That is why you haven't been pursued. It is why my little pets haven't devoured you—yet."

He paused like a man who had just remembered something. "I should give them a little reward. I know—how about Daniel?"

Ambrosi uncrossed his arms and extended a hand in Daniel's direction. Something lifted Daniel and held him in mid-air, hovering before Brenda's horrified gaze.

I was on my feet a second later. A half-second after that I was flat on my back. Chad charged, then flipped backward. No one was getting close to Ambrosi.

The unseen force moved Daniel backward over the ice. He struggled. Called for help. He screamed in a way that melted my soul like a candle in a hot oven.

"Nooooo!" Brenda screamed. Then she doubled over as if she had been punched in the gut by a prize fighter. An instant later she flew backward, falling head first onto the hard ice of the corridor. She moaned and lifted her arms to shield her head.

I couldn't stay down. I had to save Daniel even if it killed me. Which it probably would—

The first loud bang nearly burst my eardrums and for a moment I thought the ceiling was caving in. Then I heard another. And another. One bang followed the other without hesitation.

Zeke stood like a man with a steel rod for a spine. In his extended hand he held his pistol, firing shot after shot. I turned in time to see four rounds strike Ambrosi: two in the head, two in the chest.

His eyes were wide.

His mouth hung open.

He toppled backward like a board, killed as much by his pride as by Zeke's weapon.

A chorus of screeches erupted behind us. The angry eels were headed our way: some through the ice; some wriggling over the surface ice.

Zeke lowered his weapon. "We need to go...Tank, what are you doing?"

I walked to the unmoving Ambrosi, the antichrist I had brought back to life. I was meant to heal, not kill. It's my nature.

"Tank, don't." Andi found her way to her feet. Chad propped her up. "He'll never change. He's evil wrapped in flesh."

I took another step toward the corpse on the ice. Blood oozed from his wounds and steamed in the cold. Some was already freezing.

"Please, Tank," Brenda begged. "Leave him be. He tried to kill Daniel."

My hands grew warm, then hot inside my gloves. I removed one. My right hand emitted a golden glow and steam rose from it like a kettle on a stove.

I expected the others to try to prevent me from doing what I did in China, but they didn't move. "I'm ... I'm a healer. I'm ... "

I looked down and saw the open eyes of the man who would have killed us, the man who abused Andi and Brenda and Chad and would have fed Daniel to the eels.

"May God forgive me," I said, "and if He doesn't . . . I'll understand."

I left the dead man dead and turned to Brenda and Chad. Maybe there was still some healin' I could do. Before I could take two steps, the golden glow paled then disappeared. Again I had lost control of my gift. That, or what Brenda sketched was meant to be. Either way, I was brokenhearted.

We started to run. I glanced back and looked at Ambrosi again. He was covered in squirming ice eels.

Chapter 9

MAD DASH

We were on the move, trying to outrun ice-eels and get the job done before someone else showed up to kill us. Zeke led the way. Chad helped Brenda, who was still woozy.

Andi said she could manage to keep up. "He hit me in the face. I don't run with my face." That pretty,

pretty face had a swollen jaw.

I carried Daniel. Brenda insisted, and I wasn't going to argue with that girl. I had enough bruises for one trip.

A hundred or so frantic paces later the ice gave way to concrete. Zeke led us another hundred feet down the concrete corridor, then stopped and knelt on the frost-topped cement.

"Let's see the little buggers swim through concrete," Zeke said.

I set Daniel down. The kid had grown a good bit since I first met him.

Zeke slipped off his backpack. "Okay, this is where things get dangerous."

"Really?" Chad said. "What's it been so far?"

Zeke chuckled. "You're right. This is where it gets *really* dangerous."

"I can't do much more," Brenda said. "I'm all in. My head is splittin'. I'm gettin' double vision."

Zeke looked at me and I looked at him. Neither one of us liked what we heard. I was no brain surgeon, but I had seen enough football injuries to know about concussions and skull fractures.

"We'll take care of it, girl," Andi said. "You just stay on your feet."

Daniel was clinging to Brenda. She ran her fingers through his hair.

Zeke kept rummaging through his backpack. "Tank, much of this is going to fall on you. So here's what we're gonna do." He pulled several explosive charges from his pack. They looked like small radios taped to gray bricks. "Take these. I need to rest."

I stared at the contraptions. "What am I gonna do with those? I don't know how to work them."

"Chad, Andi, bring it in. You need to know this too— just in case Tank is unable to pull it off."

I looked at Andi. "He means if I buy the farm."

"Yeah, we got his drift," Chad said.

Zeke sighed. "These are easy to use. They're specially designed to be idiot proof."

I waited for Chad to make his usual snide remark about my intelligence, but he didn't take his shot. That's when I knew he was more scared than he'd ever been.

Zeke carried on. "There are two green buttons. To arm the detonator, they must be pressed at the same time. Pressing one won't do it. That's to keep accidents from happening. After you press the buttons, you have only a few minutes to find cover."

"What's the red button for?" I asked.

"It's red for a reason, Tank. Press that and you have thirty seconds to get rid of it. It's a last-ditch measure. Got it?"

"I got it, but what do you want me to do with these?"

Zeke's eyes were deadly serious. "I want you to save the team. You're going to head for the only door that leads out of this place and blow it open. It's the big, eye-shaped portal you saw on the satellite maps Andi scrounged up. These are shaped charges. That means all the force is going to go in one direction. The blast will go into the doors, not the other way. That will keep you from killing yourself. Maybe."

"After the doors blow, then what?"

"Then you're going to dash out of this place."

"We'll freeze out there," Andi said.

Zeke shook his head. "I gave that some thought before we left. Nearly all the research stations in the vicinity have seismographs to monitor earthquakes and ice quakes. People monitor those readings around the clock. The blast will get their attention, and there's no confusing an explosion from an earthquake. They'll send help."

"You sure these will get their attention?" Chad asked.

"If those don't, these will." He patted his backpack. "I got the big boys in here."

"How will I find the exit to the surface?" I asked.

Zeke pulled a wire from his backpack and let it dangle out the side. The wire was attached to a push button. His detonator.

Chad had gone as white as the ice. "Are you—what are you going to do?"

"I'm gonna bring this place down." Zeke slipped his arms through the straps of his pack. "This is the Gate's base of operations. We just need to find the nerve center."

"They'll still have another base in space," Chad said. "The one I saw on one of my bilocation trips."

"We know we can't wipe them off the face of the earth, but we can set them back a few years. Don't worry about the mothership. We're taking out this base."

"What if Azazel shows up again?" Andi sounded tired. She had a right to be. We all did.

"Leave him to me."

"Leave him to you?" Chad said. "What can you do to him? We can't stand up to him; we can't kill him; we can't defeat him."

Zeke ignored the question. "We need to go."

***

Chad and Andi helped Brenda along. Zeke and I moved down the corridor looking in every nook and cranny for anything that looked like a command center.

We discovered more storage rooms. In one compartment, we found what looked like a laboratory in one of those horror shows that tries to pass itself off as sci-fi. There were fluid-filled tanks holding some of the creatures we had seen on our earlier missions. We also saw variations of the ice-eels. These were bigger and their teeth looked like they could chew through steel. Gnawing through a person would be no problem. Chad would never have survived those bites.

More disturbing than the hybrid eels was a set of utility shelves with large jars filled with heads—dear God, just the heads—of the black-eyed children we encountered in Florida while visiting Andi's grandparents. These faces looked different. The eyes appeared almost normal, more human.

I knew that couldn't be good. They were making modifications to the hybrid children. The idea was enough to turn my stomach.

A few doors down, we found a room that looked like it belonged in the control center of NASA.

"This has to be it," Zeke said.

I took a look around. The place was filled with monitors showing different parts of the world. Some of the on-screen images looked familiar.

"Shouldn't there be people here?" Andi asked.

"Who knows?" I said. "Maybe Azazel's minions work here. Maybe... I have no idea." There are always more questions than answers.

"That's my grandparent's house!" Andi pointed to one monitor. "They've been watching us, probably for months."

"That's our hotel." Chad pointed to an image of the hotel we were using as our headquarters. Then he bent forward and worked at drawing a breath.

"What's wrong?" I asked. I looked at the places where the eels had bitten him. It was hard to tell much through the torn fabric of his Antarctic gear. I could see dark fluid staining the material, and a trail of blood marked the floor beneath us. All this time, he had been helping Brenda when he needed help just as badly. "Chad, we have to stop the bleeding—"

"Isn't this lovely." The voice came from an area of shadows near the back of the large chamber. "We're all here together. I've been waiting for you."

The figure of Azazel emerged into the light of the room. He shook his massive head. "I saw what you did to poor Ambrosi. He was our chosen one, you know. We had big plans for him. But he had a bit of an ego. Then again, who doesn't?" The giant angel moved slowly across the room.

I've faced some pretty big guys on the football field, but all of them were tiny compared to this dude. Give the Hulk pale skin instead of green, wrap him in a brown robe, give him a hairy chin, and add a finger to each hand, then you'd have this guy. Except the Hulk was still basically human. Like most angels in the Bible, Azazel had a human form, but there was nothing human about him.

"I've been around since, well, creation, and I don't think I've met a more annoying band of people. Oh, the apostles were irritating, of course, but they were someone else's problem." He paused for dramatic effect. "You, however, are *my* problem."

Then things got really weird. Here we were, a thousand feet below the ice of Antarctica, facing an evil angel giant, having survived cold, ice-eels, frozen Nazis, and storerooms of things that have haunted us since we first got together. We had fought and killed the antichrist, and seen a dear friend murdered—how could things get weirder than that?

But they did.

I turned my attention to Zeke, who slipped out of his backpack and set it near one of the walls, as casually as he would take off his pajamas and toss 'em in the dirty clothes hamper. He pressed the button on the wire that dangled from his pack.

"Tank, it's go time."

That's when he stopped being Zeke the navy guy and became Zeke the I-don't-know-what. I could guess, though. As I watched him expand to a slightly smaller version of Azazel, I assumed he was an angel. A righteous, obedient angel. There's a verse in the Bible about people entertaining angels without knowing it.

That sort of sums it all up.

"You!" Azazel said, smiling in disbelief. "Well, aren't you clever, you—"

Zeke didn't wait for Azazel to finish his sentence. Clearly, he had not come to chat. He was on Azazel before I could blink. The two careened through the room, knocking over equipment and monitors. It was almost too much to believe.

Zeke had one more thing to say, and he said it to me: "Tank! Run. Now."

The power in his voice shook me out of my trance. I spun and headed for the door. The others followed, but it was clear that Brenda was in a bad way. I hoisted her onto my shoulder in a fireman's carry. Chad looked like he was declining fast. I don't know if he was bleeding out from the eel bites or if those things had poison in their heads. At the moment, it didn't matter.

"I got him," Andi said. She did her best to serve as a human crutch for Chad. He smiled. Maybe he was trying to flirt. He finally had his arm around Andi.

Or maybe he was just in pain.

"Daniel," Brenda said. It sounded more like a sigh that a word.

"I'm here, Mom. I'm good. I can run."

We covered a dozen yards before we stopped.

"Duch," Daniel said.

I was lowering Brenda to the ice when I spotted the four black-masked humanoids we had met when we first saw Azazel. They watched us for a second, then sprinted at us.

Then past us.

They had no interest in me or the others. "They're going to help their master," I said. Why bother with us? As far as they knew, we were trapped. They could grab us later—unless Zeke's plan worked.

"Did I see what I think I saw back there?" Chad's voice was growing weaker.

"Shut up, Chad." Andi started forward again, dragging Chad with her. "Save your energy."

"Yes, ma'am." Weak and delirious, he tried to salute. We were running uphill, but our situation was going downhill.

A lot of screaming behind us as Zeke bought us some time. I repositioned Brenda on my shoulder and continued down the corridor.

We were attempting the impossible and had no time to do it in, but still we had to try. One thing I had learned about our team: if we went down, we would go down fighting.

Twenty yards ahead I saw our goal: a massive set of black doors shaped like a giant eye.

I stopped at ten yards out. I was going to have to blow the doors like Zeke said and we couldn't be too close when that happened.

When I set Brenda down, she didn't move an inch. I could see her chest rise and fall, but her eyes were at half-mast.

Tears trickled down my face. I told myself I didn't have time to imagine the worst right now. That didn't keep my brain from doing it as I ran toward the doors.

I worked as fast as I could. Zeke's backpack of death was on a timer. He only had to keep Azazel and his goons away from it until it blew. I had no idea what an explosion would do to other worldly beings, but I did know what it would do the likes of me and the others if I messed this up.

I placed the directional charges where I thought they'd do most good and ran back to the others.

"Huddle up." I turned my back to the door, pulled Brenda in front of me. Daniel sat in front of her. Andi did her best to shelter Chad.

The explosion shook my everything. Ears rang. Heat rushed over us. The corridor was concrete, but a thin layer of ice covered everything. It fell around us like broken glass.

"Talk to me." My voice sounded strange in my ears.

"I'm okay." Andi didn't sound so sure.

"My ears hurt again," Daniel said.

No one else spoke. Not good.

I stood. "Outside, Daniel. Go now."

"Mom. Mom."

"Go, little buddy. I'll get her. Go."

He did.

"You too, Andi."

"I can't lift Chad. I need help."

"Get out. I'll come back for him. Go."

"I can't—"

"Don't argue!"

She stepped to me and kissed me. And for one moment I wasn't freezing, busted up Tank. I was just the luckiest man in the world.

Andi pulled away and ran for the opening.

I picked up Brenda, but I had to make three attempts. I was spent. I was broken. I staggered out the portal and lay Brenda on the ice. She looked bad. I made the trip back inside to get Chad. I couldn't lift him, so I used the last of my strength to drag him outside and set him beside Brenda.

He wasn't breathing.

Neither was she.

Daniel was on his knees, his head resting on Brenda's chest. Crying came first. Then deep weeping. Then wailing, as only a broken-hearted boy can.

Andi knelt beside him and sobbed.

Daniel struggled to speak through his grief.

Soft words.

Powerful words.

"Best . . . mom . . . ever."

Another explosion rocked the earth. A big one. Zeke's backpack—the one with the "big boys"—had gone off. Ice and concrete dust blew through the open door, showering us with debris. Andi, who was closest to Daniel, threw her body over the boy.

When everything settled, the door we had passed through was gone, replaced by a deep depression in the ice. Giant chunks of ice lay where once a smooth surface had been.

"Zeke did it," I said. "I don't know how he did it, but he did it."

The cracked ice moved as if something was pushing up from below.

Andi stared at the moving earth. "This is never going to end, is it?"

Again, I struggled to my feet, swaying where I stood. The ice sheet continued to rumble, making standing ever more difficult.

Azazel appeared in the heaps of ice. Don't ask how—I had no idea. I had no idea how he did any of the things I'd seen him do.

"You, Man of Faith. You did this to my sanctuary." He was not offering congratulations, and it took a second for me to realize he was talking to me.

I met his gaze. Despite the pain, I managed to grin. "Actually, I only helped."

"You have annoyed me far too long." He started coming my way, and I realized he wasn't walking. He was floating just above the ice. "You and that boy." He pointed at Daniel.

I steeled myself for a confrontation, but who was I kidding? I was too busted up to offer much of a fight. Even Daniel could take me out in the first round. Still, I would stand my ground. I couldn't let him win.

Azazel was on me before I could blink. He caught me by the throat and lifted me in the air. I cut my eyes to the side and realized I was a good thirty feet above the surface.

I said at the beginning that this would be the story of my death. Brenda's picture showed all of us dead except Daniel. Sometimes her drawings were more like warnings than prophecies, but I had known in my heart and that this would be my last stand.

So be it.

I seized Azazel's throat as he had seized mine, but I had too little strength, and I doubted it would do any good. But if I couldn't be victorious, at least I could be defiant. I tried to squeeze and managed to make the fiend smile.

"First you," he said. "Then your pretty friend. Then I'm going to torture the boy to death. I promise to take my time with him."

He threw me toward the sharp-edged ice. Tossed me like I was a rag doll. He was more than a match for me. He was a match for a hundred of me.

I landed on my back. I heard a loud, gut-wrenching snap as my upper body bent one way and my lower body another. I'm not sure how I remained conscious. Fear, probably. I could move my head and my arms, but not my legs. He broke my back.

Breathing grew difficult. I could hear myself wheezing.

Then I felt a thud next to me. Andi landed on the ice, face down. Andi. My sweet, sweet Andi moved her head just enough to see me. Our eyes met. I saw no fear in her eyes, only her love. I hope she could see the love I felt for her.

I was losing my ability to move my head, so I had to rely on my hearing for the rest of the story.

"Enough!" Zeke's voice rang out, bigger and

badder.

"The boy will be mine." That was Azazel.

"No, he is not and you know it. I am his protector, and I will fight you from now until the end of eternity if I have to. He is special. He is chosen."

Azazel roared. The sound thundered across the ice.

Then I heard another sound—the steady chop, chop, chop of a helicopter. Daniel would be safe.

"Come here, little buddy." I croaked out the words and Daniel obeyed. Tears had iced up on his face.

"Remember something . . ." My breath caught. I had only moments. "Every ending is a beginning. Got it?"

"Yes, Tank. I got it."

"Say it for me, buddy."

"Every ending is a beginning."

"My man. You da best, ever."

"No." The tears began to pour. "No, *you* da best, ever."

"Keep the faith, buddy. Keep the faith."

"I will, Tank."

I managed a weak nod. "I need a favor. My glove. Take it off."

He loosened, then removed my right glove. Cold air stung my flesh. I shifted my gaze to Andi. She didn't speak. I don't think she could, but she did blink a few times. I took that to mean *yes.*

"Now Andi's."

Daniel figured it out. He removed her glove and gently placed our hands together.

We held hands—no gloves—and together we crossed the threshold.

Epilogue

DAN

The needle bit into my skin. I could feel its bite up and down my right arm. That was to be expected and I made no complaints. I had other issues to deal with: my emotions.

"You doing okay, kid?"

The tattoo artist had a bald head, no eyebrows, and tattoos up his neck and the side of his head. An epic beard hung from his chin, and his breath was slightly sour, like stale beer.

"I'm fine."

I tried not to look at the tattoo, my first. I had waited eight years to get this. I was eighteen now; almost nineteen. I've spent a good part of the last decade living in Florida with Andi's grandparents.

They've taken good care of me. They even arranged for home schooling. Go figure. I don't fit in well at a regular school. The professor left his money to me, so I'm pretty well off. At least I was never a burden to my new grandparents. They cried over Andi a lot. We shared our tears. It seemed to help some.

Eight years have passed since that day in the Antarctic. Eight years since I was loaded on a helicopter and flown to McMurdo. Eight years is a long time, but not long enough for me to forget the sight of my friends—no, more than friends. They were family.

I left their bodies on the ice. That sounds horrible, but I knew they were no longer there. I saw them go.

As long as I can remember, I've seen the unseen world. Not perfectly. None of our gifts worked perfectly, probably because perfect gifts have trouble functioning in imperfect people.

My gift worked pretty good as I was being led to the chopper. Behind me rested the bodies of the only people on the planet I was capable of loving, but a short distance away, in a place no one else could see, was a scene bathed in gold light. The ice and the cold had been wiped away by the warmth there. The kind of warm that is inside and outside a person.

In the gold mist, I saw a line of people. Smiling people. Whole, undamaged people. Tank waved. Andi blew me a kiss. Chad raised a fist to his chest and thumped his sternum—his way of saying, "Love ya, kid."

I saw the professor, too. Looking younger and stronger. I couldn't tell he had been crucified a thousand feet below the ice.

And then there was my mom. Adoptive or not, she was and will forever be Mom. She looked up and crossed her arms over her chest as if hugging me. She seemed happy. She seldom showed happiness. She had fought too many battles in her tough life, but she looked joyful in that golden glow.

It's that view of heaven that keeps me sane, that keeps me from waking up screaming every night. I replay that scene a hundred times a day. It gets me out of bed in the morning and encourages me to think of the future.

I saw something else on that trip: a vision of a star falling from space, a star I understood to be the Gate's orbital mothership, the thing Chad had seen on one of his soul projection trips. It's somewhere at the bottom of the ocean now. What's left of it, that is.

"Uh, oh." The tat man swore. "I did it again."

My heart sank. "Did you ruin it?" I didn't want to look.

"Look kid . . . sometimes I ink something and I don't know why. I've followed the picture of the tattoo you gave me but..."

I had given him a photo of the tattoo my mom inked on Tank's arm so long ago. She had done the work in this very shop, and there was a good chance

Tank had sat in this very chair.

"But what?"

"Here." He handed me a mirror. "This will make it easier to see."

I looked at the image on my arm. My skin was red and a little swollen, but everything was clear enough to see. There was my mom's face, dreadlocks and all; Andi looked real enough to crawl off my arm. The professor and Tank were as lifelike as could be. Chad was inked to one side. The artist had to add him from a photo I had. It all looked right to me...

Then I saw it. He had added another person: Zeke. Zeke my protector, my guardian angel.

"It's okay," I said. "Believe it or not, I know him."

"I believe it. This happens more than I like to admit. Too many drugs when I was young." He took the mirror from me. "I'm sorry. I'll pay for the tat."

"No need," I said. "It's perfect."

"But—"

"My mom used to work here when I was little. She used to do the same thing. So it's cool. No worries."

He nodded in appreciation and finished up a few rough spots. He then put some plastic wrap over his latest work of art. I slipped from the chair and paid the man. I gave him a pretty good tip. Again, thanks to the professor.

I started for the door.

"Thanks for understanding," the tat man said. "Hey, you never told me your name."

I opened the door and stood at the threshold. "It's Dan—Daniel Barnick." Then, for some unclear reason, I added, "I'm the last Harbinger."

The warm Southern California night enveloped me and some of Tank's last words played in my head:

"Every ending is a beginning."

END GAME

fini

About Alton L. Gansky

Alton L. Gansky (Al) is the author of fifty works of book length fiction and nonfiction. He has been a Christy Award finalist (*A Ship Possessed*) and an Angel Award winner (*Terminal Justice*) and recently received the ACFW award for best suspense/thriller for his work on *Fallen Angel*. He holds a BA and MA in biblical studies and was granted a Litt.D. He lives in central California with his wife.

www.altongansky.com

CPSIA information can be obtained
at www.ICGtesting.com
Printed in the USA
LVOW03s1505040617
536877LV00008B/754/P